THE CAVE MAGE
WIZARD WARRIOR QUEST

C.A.A. ALLEN

Fantastic Science Fantasy Adventures Press

If you purchased this book without a cover, you should be aware that this book is stolen property. It was reported as "unsold and destroyed" to the publisher, and neither the author nor the publisher has received any payment for this "stripped book."

No part of this publication may be reproduced, stored in a retrieval system, or transmitted in any form or by any means, electronic, mechanical, photocopying, recording, or otherwise, except for the use of brief quotations in a book review.

This is a work of fiction. All characters within are the products of the authors imagination. Any resemblance to actual persons, living or dead, is entirely coincidental and all incidents are pure invention.

ISBN-10: 0-69246-672-X

ISBN-13: 978-0-69246-672-8

Copyright © 2015 by C. A. A. Allen. All rights reserved.

Published by

Fantastic Science Fantasy Adventures Press

1 Bagshot Row, Hobbiton, Nottinghamshire,

NG9 1BS, United Kingdom

First Edition: July 2015

Book designed by Master IAM of Zwolle Ltd, St Ives Plc

Cover, maps, & illustrations by Darko Tomic

Dungeon maze layout by Master of the Playing Cards

For Christopher II, LaSkyeya, Naleesa, C. KaeShawn, Lelia, Angelina, and Antonio - my children are my strength.

"Just as treasures are uncovered from the earth, so virtue appears from good deeds, and wisdom appears from a pure and peaceful mind. To walk safely through the maze of human life, one needs the light of wisdom and the guidance of virtue."

- Buddha

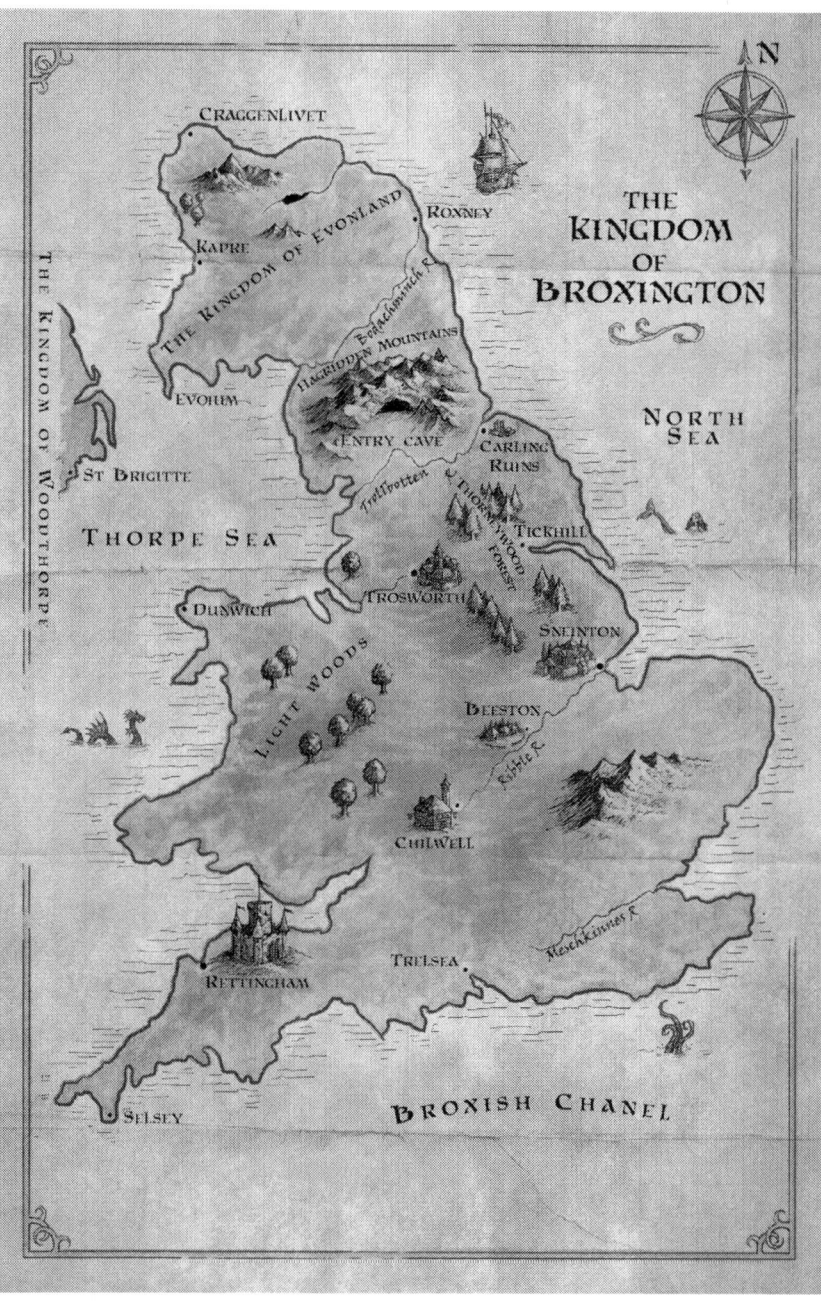

PART ONE

"THE TEAM"

CHAPTER 1

The pub owner jumped on top of a table near the center hearth. "Listen up! The odds makers have a new favorite for the scholarship, a young man who can swing a sword with the best." He pointed at me. "Raff Jenkins!"

The pub erupted with high-spirited cheers. I folded my arms and leaned against the rough-carved bar like it was no big deal. The bartender lined three more cups of honey mead in front of me. Couldn't beat free. Just as I almost had the first one to my lips, a raving drunk smashed his cup into it.

The man smiled from ear to ear. "Cheers, young sword slinger. You passed that magic user to become the two-to-one favorite, but I am not going to place my bet on you. Fighters don't win these things. Tomorrow, when they announce the *magic* user as the winner, I'm going to be four times as rich as I am now. Four-to-one odds on a magic user. Now that's a bet."

With any luck, *I'd* be four times as rich, and finally able to pay this months' rent. I rapid fire drank all three meads and slammed the final cup on the bar. "You're wrong. The Mondovi scholarship will be mine."

A set of silky smooth hands wrapped around my arm and pulled me off my seat. Vixenett swayed from side to side, her cheeks rosy and smile bright. "Let's get out of here, Raff. We can celebrate at your place."

Now *that* sounded like my kind of celebration.

The bartender reached across the bar and grabbed my other arm. "You aren't taking him anywhere Mabel! The birthday boy can't leave yet. The Skeppers Pub rule is one drink for every year of life, and he's only had sixteen. Raff's got two more drinks coming."

Vixenett pulled me toward the door on the other side of the room. "Sorry, Thorvald. This party is going private. And you know better than to call me by my birth name."

We weaved past the stained tables of gamblers, stepping over some dropped dice and spilled mead. A flash of the hearth fire flickered in the eve-darkened windows just before we stepped outside.

Once in the crisp night air, we held hands and stumbled in what I thought was the general direction of my cabin. "I can definitely use another drink. It's the rule, you know. Did Thorvald call you Mabel?" I tried to focus on Vixenett but it was no use. The heavy consumption of mead had made everything a blur. The last thing I remembered was falling into bed.

⚔ ⚔ ⚔

Several heavy thumps on my door woke me. *Not the landlord again.*

I sat up. The room spun, wobbled, and came to a stop. The morning sun pierced through the crack under my door. I looked around. My sword lay dangerously in the middle of the floor, and clothes littered my hazard table, the only piece of furniture in my rickety one-room home.

I gently pulled back the covers to get a look at my houseguest. Vixenett's coppery auburn hair splayed across both pillows. Seeing her in my bed made me smile. We'd spent a lot of time together lately. Some would say we were dating. I slowly ran my finger down her arm when the assault on my door began again. The violent knock shook one of the hinges off the door. Vixenett rolled over and put a pillow over her head.

My brain felt like it was going to explode into at least a million pieces. With my senses starting to come back, I recognized the knocking pattern. Three quick, three slow, and one loud pound.

Dread was the only person who would do this.

"Wait, damn you!" I slipped on my leather boots, wrapped a tattered blanket around my waist, and stumbled to the door. "There better be a whole lot of gold to be made at the shop to get me up this early."

The knocking got even louder. I covered my ears. "Why you so impatient, Dread? Hold on, it's way too early for all that noise."

I cracked open my creaky wooden door and peeked outside. Yellow, red, and orange leaves blew in with a brisk cold gust. Even in autumn, the dirt road from town to my cabin still looked dry and dusty.

I took in the short human interruption bouncing up and down on his toes. "You ready to open up the shop, old man Jenkins?" He tried to push his way in, but I blocked him.

Even though our fathers were brothers, it would be difficult to see the family resemblances between Dread and me. He had a darker complexion and was shorter than me. I did my best to keep my hair combed and smelling decent. Dread's hair was always a thick, curly, tangled rat's nest and currently reeked of exotic herb smoke.

"Old man Jenkins?" I said. "Last I checked, I was younger than you, cousin."

"Oh yah?" Dread said. "Sure you right."

"Why you here at this ungodly time of morning anyway? We never open up the shop this early."

"You overslept, the sorry-ass questers will be returning from the Cave Maze any time now, drunky. The High Road is already getting crowded, and we got busters to sell. There's also the matter of a scholarship announcement that I know you don't want to miss."

I smack my palm into my forehead. How could I have overslept on the biggest day of my life? The day I'd take my first steps out of this sleepy, snake pit of a village. I'll never drink again if I win this scholarship. Never again. "Thank you for being an early bird, cousin."

Dread made a few obnoxious sniffing noises. He looked over my shoulder with one eyebrow raised. "Hey, Raff," he whispered. "I didn't know you had company. Who that you laid up with?"

I looked back in my room to confirm Vixenett was still sound asleep. "The owner of that curvy silhouette you see in my bed is none of your business. It just belongs to the sexiest, coolest, and most loveliest young thing I know." I took a few steps back and pulled a curtain in front of the bed. "We had some late evening crisples and milk, ya know. But enough about my girl, let me get ready to go."

As I dressed in brown wool trousers, a deerskin vest, and a thick overcoat, Dread picked clothes off my hazard table and flung them to the floor. He kept Vixenett's undergarments at a distance, pinching and tossing them into my curtain. He then selected two dice from the five kept in a semicircular wooden tray, and rolled them across the layout of the hazard table. They landed, showing a total of three.

"Three is a losing roll on the come out," I said. "How's your dice arm now days? You know, it's always better—"

"—to finesse the dice," Dread cut in. "I know, I know. I haven't forgot my father's advice."

"Famous advice," I corrected.

Dread pulled two dice from his pocket. "It's a whole lot easier to finesse the dice when you have these." He was careful to set the dice with the three spots in a V on top, and then lightly threw them down low, with almost no arc. They landed, showing a total of seven, a come out winner.

Dread snapped his fingers and pointed at me. "I can roll damn near any number I want with *these* bones."

"You still carry around those weighted dice Uncle Mack made?" It might have been best for him had he lost them. As perfect as those cheating tools were, they could be dangerous nowadays.

"Yes, sir. A lot of gold has been swindled with these gems. One time, my father went on a road trip, leaving me at home with nothing but the raggedy clothes on my back and these dice in my hand. He told me to earn my keep while he was gone, and that I did. When he returned to the village, I had a fur-lined coat, a cornucopia of fruit, and a sack of herbs bigger than your head. So yeah, I still carry these dice."

That sounded exactly like something Uncle Mack would do, but just for banter's sake... "Uncle Mack did not do that to you."

"Yes he did. We should bring the hustle back. Our fathers taught us the game way too well to let these skills go to waste."

Tempting as it was, I had a scholarship coming to me with a bright future. "The Hazard scam was one of the sweetest our dads ever came up with, but those crooked dice will get you killed. House dice are the standard at gambling dens now, the hustle wouldn't work these days."

I picked up and sheathed my sword. How did this end up on the floor? I pulled back the curtain, kissed Vixenett on her forehead, then gave Dread a wink. "Mmm, Mmm, Mmm, I just might have to marry this one. Let's go!"

CHAPTER 2

Dread and I squeezed our way through the crowd to open for business. Our one-room shop rose like a boulder amidst the river of people. Spectators lined the road, end-to-end, in some places five deep.

"It looks like the whole village came out today, except the drunks at the Skepp." I spot Questing University's Chancellor Liberi and his entourage schmoozing their way to the stage on the outskirts of town. "Look, Dread. There goes the man that's going to grant me that scholarship."

Dread flicked his hand and looked the other direction. "Damn Liberi, he isn't giving me anything. And there's no guarantee he's giving you anything either. None at all."

After plenty of elbowing, we reached our shop. I stood tall and continued. "The current line on me is two-to-one, cousin. That does make me the favorite. My dream of attending Questing University is coming to fruition."

"I don't know what you expect to learn from those stuck-up phonies." Dread grinned and leaned against the wall of our shop. "You're already the best in village with a sword."

That was the point. I didn't want to be the best in the village. I wanted to be the best in the kingdom…in *all* skills. Not just swordplay. "Well, on top of bettering the swordsmanship that I already know, I'll be learning knife fighting, archery, spear work, burglary, and safebreaking from the best."

"What?" Dread lurched back to a standing position. "Did you say burglary and safebreaking? I can teach you everything you need to know about those subjects. I must have watched my dad break into a thousand chests, difficult ones too. People from all over Broxington used to pay him to open them. My father never set off a single trap, and he always got the treasure out unscathed. He taught me how to do it too. I'm damn good."

"I know, but the university also teaches the arts, law, and medicine. Things you know nothing about."

Dread scrunched his lips. "I don't care about that stuff."

"After graduating, I will be in demand with the top paying questing teams entering the Cave Maze. Top paying, Dread. I can't wait."

The crowd spread in front of us. "Watch out there now! Coming through." An old man whipped a walking cane from side to side, hitting people on their ankles.

"It's old man Bendigo," Dread said. "Your biggest fan. I don't know why you like this guy."

"I like him because he was the only one to bet I would be victorious in my first abbey tournament, and he did it when I was a thirty-to-one freshman dog." I flicked my collar. "You know I beat three upperclassmen in first round victories to win that thing. Bendigo cheered me on all the way, and slid several gold coins my direction after the victory. You're just mad you didn't follow his bet."

"My boy Raff!" Bendigo rasped. "Your sword skills are the best I have seen since Giovanni Mondavi himself! A lot of these boobs throwing down gold on that sissified magic user and bougie fighter you up against, but they ain't 'bout nothin'. I got my gold bet on you at the Skepp, son. I'm on my way there right now."

"Well you fixing to be a rich man, Bendigo," I said. "I'd appreciate a toke after that payout."

He continued down the street waving a finger in the air. "I got you, boy! I got you!"

I folded my arms and grinned. This could end up being the best day of my life. Bendigo knows, magic users are *not* all that great.

Dread unlocked our shop door and kicked over a rock to hold it open. Before stepping in, he pulled a pin from a tiny hole in the wall, and scrutinized the ceiling. After disengaging the boulder and acid globe trap his father had designed, he walked in.

I hoisted the large wooden panel at our main window and propped it up with a stick. All eight businesses surrounding the village square were busy.

My old friend Gibbet loitered around begging people to buy his oxymel, a honey and vinegar drink used for the treatment of fever, pain, or whatever else the peddler thinks they need to say to sell the swill. Now that was just sad. Gibbet actually had some good fighting skills back in the day. It would be living death to be him, stuck here peddling honey-related products in the streets.

Dread pried a slat off our bench seat, lifted out a chest and opened it. Inside were four small brown corncobs with string tails, the last of our highly coveted chest-buster explosives in the inventory.

Dread kicked the bottom of the bench. "Only four busters to sell and we're bone dry."

Four? That was it? On a day like today, we needed at least a dozen.

A slender man with a belette on his shoulder approached the shop. Aw man, I wanted a belette, also called a sniffer. Some people called them common weasels, but I knew better. Belettes could sniff out any harm that could ruin a quester's day in the Maze—traps, curses, spells, and the presence of evil and magic were just a few of the things a well-trained belette could warn of.

Four lousy busters wouldn't make enough gold to purchase a belette's toenail. But maybe winning the scholarship would set me up enough to get one.

The man stepped in our shop and adjusted his leather sword belt, it had several knives, and a simple flanged mace suspended from it. "Do you sell potions?"

I picked up a buster and presented it to the quester. "No potions. We only sell chest-busters here. They're a must-have if you're going in the Maze."

His belette jumped down to a table. Colored reddish brown with a white underbelly, it stood up on its hind legs. Maybe I'd get one like that.

"Who is this?" I rested my elbows on the counter, peering as closely at the belette as I could without inciting a reprimand.

The belette's little pink nose twitched, it sniffed and looked around the shop rapidly.

The man lifted his chin. "Her name is Tavi. She can sense a hag from across forest and hills."

I gave her a light pet under the chin. "A fine looking sniffer." She started dooking—a chuckling bark—licked my hand, and then jumped down to explore the shop.

Yup. I'd get myself a sniffer the moment I got that scholarship gold.

The man held the chest-buster at both ends and gave it a half twirl. "Exquisitely rolled." He brought it up to his nose and took a whiff. His face turned sour as he pulled it away. "Skunky, does this have huo-yao in it?"

Dread leaned forward and made strong eye contact with the man. "The best explosives always do. That and a few secret ingredients make our chest-busters the best."

The man held the buster out toward Dread. "My team has a thief, and a magic user to open chests."

Dread pushed the explosive back. "There are some chests in the Maze that will baffle even the most skilled of thieves. Chests so well fortified that your team will have to leave them down there unopened. You'll always be haunted with the thought of what could have been in it."

"That's a good point," I said. "And as far as magic users go, only a foolish questing captain would waste their precious spell power to open a chest."

"A chest-buster can make you a hero, my man," Dread said. "When a chest's lock is too difficult, or time consuming for your thief to crack, the chest-buster will come in handy. These explosives deliver a strong and precise blast with minimum noise. Just place it on the chest and pull the string. Our chest-busters will blow the lock clean off that thing with no harm to the treasures inside. For five gold coins you can be your team's hero."

The man smoothed his mustache. "Since you put it that way, I'll take one."

"Just one?" I tossed a second in the air and caught it.

His eyes followed the movement, but he shook his head. "Just one today."

As he walked away, I toyed with the explosive. "Our fathers' greatest invention. Uncle Mack does a great job of crafting these things. We've made a whole lot of gold off of this product right here."

"Our fathers' great invention won't be making us gold for much longer," Dread said. "Our inventory has never been this low before. If your dad's connection doesn't come through with more huo-yao soon, we are going to be out of business."

"Let's not count on my father for any more huo-yao. We can find someone else to buy it from." Frankly, we couldn't count on my dad for anything. He was the most unreliable man in Broxington.

"The store in Trosworth is our only alternative," Dread said. "If Moe has it in stock, he charges three hundred gold coins per sack."

"But my dad gets those same sacks for thirty! Moe buys our chest-busters from you for re-sale. He should give us the supplier discount."

"I do have a good rapport with Moe, but he does *not* do discounts on huo-yao. If your father doesn't come through, we're sunk."

It wasn't my fault that my father left us hanging. I'd wasted too many hours arguing with him to get it together and to deliver. It was up to him to hold up his end of a bargain.

But this situation wouldn't bring me down. Not today. This was my day.

I scooted out of our door and took a long look up the road. "The questers should be here any time now."

Dread peered out the shop window standing on his tiptoes. "I'm looking forward to this too, Raff. Hey, hey look at this boy over here." He pointed to a shifty juvenile jumping up and down in the crowd. "You ready to get some coins, Malin? I'm watching you boy."

Malin jumped on another boy's shoulders and stretched out a butterfly net. "Look at this, Dread!" The two boys teetered from side to side, whacking into people along the road. "I'm going to break your coin catching record this year. You just watch me."

Dread's mouth dropped. "Oh, that can't be done, young Malin! The only thing you're going to break is your back when you fall."

"Remember getting excited like that on quester return day?" I asked. "We caught more coins than any kid in town." Now that we had the buster shop, catching coins was child's play.

Dread laughed and nodded. "Those were some good times. We would come up big. No sign of the questers yet. Where are they?"

I leaned a shoulder against the shop. "Since when have you been so excited about the quester's return? I thought you didn't like the university's team."

Dread pulled a betting slip from his pocket. "I got a whole lot of gold bet on their death over-under number at the Skepp."

Dread and I placed a lot of death over-under bets. It was the most popular wager made on questing teams. The odds maker critiqued one's team as a whole, and predicted how many members would die on their run in the Maze. Gamblers wagered that the actual number would be either higher or lower than the number the odds maker set.

"What's the university's number?" I asked.

"Four." Dread ran his fingers across his betting slip. "Word is, the Maze has been dishing out an unhealthy dose of death on all questers entering it lately. I hope to make some gold on that inside information. This is going to be the big one, cousin."

"Look!" shouted a member of the crowd. "Look at the tree tops! Here they come everyone! Here comes the university's team!"

THE HOUNDS

CHAPTER 3

I kicked over a crate and stepped on top of it to get a better view. Just as I got steady the questing university team convoy burst through an opening in the forest. The crowd roared and jammed the road leading to our Village Square.

"Yaaaaaaa!" I unleashed a primal call. "They here Dread! They here!"

The first vessel was an elaborate four-wheeled open carriage pulled by two horses. It contained all of the team's senior questers. Three black and gold flags of death whipped in the chilly breeze. The team's senior fighter, a large man wearing plate armor, stood tall from the high outside box seat next to the driver. He thrust his fists up, nodded, and smiled as the crowd began to overrun the road.

"How many flags, Raff?" Dread clutched his betting slip like a lifeline. "How many flags?"

I hated the break the news to him, but it wasn't the first time he lost a bet. And it wouldn't be the last. "Only three. Looks like they had a clean run."

He grabbed my sleeve. "How many did you say?"

"Just three." The carriage rolled by with the crunch of wheels on grit. A reflection of sun off gold hit my eyes. "Dread, you got to see how much treasure they hauled in. Come look at this." Maybe a distraction would help soften the news.

Dread tossed both hands in the air. "Oh hell no! The death over-under at the Skepp was four. Damn, damn, damn!" He ripped the slip in half, threw the pieces to the floor, and then jumped up and down on them. "I needed that payout real bad too."

The second wagon was a tall, two-story wooden structure pulled by a team of four horses. The lower room was covered on all sides, and had portholes from which archers could fire in times of trouble. The higher room was open, and acted as a platform where several treasure chests sat displaying various coins, mainly glittering gold. It was crowded with the team's younger members, some sat with legs dangling over the edge, others stood waving. As per tradition, they all tossed silver pennies to the cheering horde.

One day I would be riding on top of that wagon. I would stand right in the front, dig my hand deep into the treasure, and then rain down coins on all the kids. Over at the Skepp I'd buy out the bar for a whole night, drinks on me. I'd probably purchase a real nice gold bracelet for Vixenett too. She'd love it.

A mob of children scrambled through the crowd in pursuit of a coin elusively rolling on its edge. An elderly woman got knocked down and shook her fist at them. Others got trampled as the swarm twisted through the bystanders.

Dread joined me on top of the crate, gripping the shop roof for balance. "Get your coins kids! I see you!" He then turned his attention to the questers throwing out the currency and started heckling. "Why don't you ho's throw out some of those gold coins for a change? Ya cheap bastards!"

"If they start throwing out gold I'm pushing you away and diving in," I said.

Dread clinched his fist. "I would have the gold in my clutch long before you got your hands on me."

Two mules brought the third and final vessel into view. The crowd went wild with cheers and sounds of awe. The flatbed wagon held a cage containing two pitch-black hellhounds, no doubt headed for Questing University's menagerie of Cave Maze monsters. The muscular beasts thrashed around the cage in a crazed rage. They wore muzzles, but still managed to spit scorching flames through them to the crowd's delight. One quester's belette got too close to the hound's fiery breath and let out a high pitched screech.

"Ha, ha!" Dread mocked. "That sniffer got its tail burnt up."

"Better its tail than its sensitive nose."

The team convoy rolled to a stop in the middle of Village Square. One of their magic users held a finger up and shot a firework out of it into the air. The multicolored globe burst into sparkling flakes that blew wildly in the wind. A few of the big flakes fluttered down to the ground where several children made an incredible effort to snatch a souvenir. One small flake drifted near by. I took a swipe at it, lost my balance, but righted myself.

Dread shook his head. "See?"

See what? Didn't everyone like souvenirs?

With a crack of the coachman's whip the convoy once again rolled on to the stage.

A rider on horseback broke off from the procession and headed toward our shop front.

Dread tapped my shoulder. "Here comes the university's buyer. I think it's my man Joe." He rubbed his hands together. "Yes, yes it is. It's my man Joe Vega. I'm in good with this guy. We should have a purchase right here. Jump down Raff."

Joseph was a scruffy, behemoth of a man with black hair and a thick, tightly twisted gray beard. A known hard fighter and questing veteran, he had been a part of the team for as long as I could remember. He came to an abrupt stop that kicked a cloud of dirt our direction.

Dread coughed and wiped dirt from his eyes. "Hello Joe."

Joseph stared at Dread from atop his horse. "I am going to need a dozen explosives."

"We only have three in stock," Dread said. "How did the Maze treat you—"

"Give me the three then!" Joseph shoveled fifteen loose gold coins from his pocket. A few bounced off of Dread's hand to the ground. "The Cave Maze was very good to me. I need to place an order for nine more explosives, I will pick them up on my way out of town in seven days."

Dread paused for a moment. "Um, I can do that, but I will need you to pre-pay at ten gold each."

Joseph clenched his fists. "Ten?" He shuffled through his things and dropped a small gold-filled bag down to Dread. "Very well then, but you two better not disappoint."

My spirits rose when that bag hit Dreads hand. Ninety gold would put us at one hundred ten for the day, making this the most profitable single day we ever had. My cut would be plenty enough to pay rent.

Dread smiled as he examined the bag's contents. "Trust me, we won't disa—"

Joseph jumped down from his horse, put Dread in a strangle hold, and held a long thin dagger to his throat. "You a silly little thief. I don't trust no one, especially a Jenkins."

I took a step back toward the bench seat where Dread kept two poison-tipped shuriken throwing spikes. I wasn't as accurate as him with the weapon, but at this distance, an overhead throw would land true.

Joseph pushed Dread away and pointed the blade at him. "You have my gold, and I absolutely must have the explosives in seven days. I'll pick them up on my way out of town at sunrise." He pointed the blade at me, and then slid it nearly across his throat. "You two do know that I am all business right? Play games with me and I will kill you both. There will be no questions asked, and no excuses listened to. I will slit both of your throats, then sit down to some hot sop in the morning."

Joseph's eyes opened wide as if a sudden rush of ice water ran through his veins. "Then, then I am going to have my real pretty wench bring me a chalice filled to the brim with top shelf honey wine, and there won't be no thoughts in my head of what I did to you two. So don't even think about hustling me. I'm back in seven days."

Joseph mounted his horse. Dread handed him our final three chest-busters in inventory. He snatched them and rode toward the stage.

"You call *that* being "in good" with the guy?" I tossed the spikes back in the bench seat.

"He was a bit skittish." Dread rubbed the back of his head.

"He was just about to receive a couple spikes to the belfry. I just need to know one thing Dread. Are you sure your dad can have nine busters ready by the time this fool comes back?"

Dread wiped a trickle of sweat from his forehead and sat on the bench. "My father can have them ready, but we only have enough huo-yao for three full-strength busters."

I rubbed my neck in thought of Joseph's threat. "But you just promised nine."

Dread sprung up with his index finger raised. "What I could do is have Joe's order cut real light, light enough to stretch the huo-yao out to the nine we need for the order."

"We can't pull that off! They won't be powerful enough to put a dent in a Cave Maze chest. Joseph and Questing University will never buy from us again when they find out the explosives are bogus." I removed the stick holding up the window panel and let it slam closed.

Dread returned the now empty chest back into the bench seat and replaced the slat. "Well your father's supplier of huo-yao has had absolutely nothing lately. According to Moe the hags have been buying up every last sack they can get their filthy hands on, and they buy regardless of price. The cost of huo-yao at Moe's is probably even higher than three hundred gold coins per sack now. We don't have nearly enough gold for that."

"We should think this over cousin. Joseph in not only the university's buyer, he's also a professor there. I'm probably going to have some interaction with him when I'm enrolled, he might even teach a class I'm going to be in." This was exactly what I strove to get away from. Living the life of a scammer who constantly feared a knife in the back. Hustling people this way had caused my family to be ridiculed for years. It was a stigma that was all going to change starting with me enrolled in the university.

"Is that all you ever think about Raff? The university this, the university that. Damn! I got another plan that will keep you in the good graces of your so-called institute of higher learning."

We stepped outside the shop. Dread locked the door, reset the booby trap and faced me. "I recently made a foolproof bet at the Skepp that's going to pay off *real* big. With the gold we just received from Joe, and my bet's payoff, we should have enough to purchase a sack of huo-yao from Moe. Then we'll be able to fulfill the order at full strength. We'll even have huo-yao remaining to make more inventory."

"So our futures, and throats, ride on one of your bets Dread?" He might've been my best friend, but sometimes I wanted to kick him in the neck. Was he really going to rely on a bet for this? Again? Hadn't he learned his lesson? "What did you make this so-called foolproof bet on anyway?"

Dread smacked his lips. "I can't tell you cousin, I don't want to jinx it."

"Well my foolproof way to stack up gold is to win this scholarship," I said. "Once I graduate from the university I'm almost guaranteed a spot on that team. Did you see those overflowing chests? All those questers come back with a healthy share of gold."

"Or dead." Dread laughed.

"Do you think I'm going to win this scholarship cousin?"

Dread pulled a betting slip from his pocket. "Hmm, let me see."

THE SKEPPERS PUB:
ODDS TO WIN THE GIOVANNI MONDOVI SCHOLARSHIP.

Raff Jenkins / 2 - 1 / Age: 18
(Human Male - Fighter)
Weapon of choice: Short sword
*Is an undefeated 16-0 in amateur competition.
*Has not faced competition outside of Beeston.
*Has yet to face the tougher competition in Rettingham.

Chazekiel Manor / 3 - 1 / Age: 18
(Human Male - Fighter)
Weapon of choice: Two-handed claymore
*Is 19-2 in amateur competition.
*Is 5-0 against amateur competition in Rettingham.
*Only two losses came at the hands of Raff Jenkins in Beeston.

Zombo Packer / 4 - 1 / Age: 17
(Human Male - Magic User)
*Excellent 80% execution rate on strike type spell.
*Meager 20% execution rate on heal type spell.
*Magic users have won three of the four Mondovi scholarships granted.

Tigress Moet / 8 - 1 /Age: 18
(Half Elf Female - Fighter)
Weapon of choice: Duel trident daggers
*Is 13-3 in amateur competition.
*All three loses due to archery bull's-eye misses.
*No female has ever won the scholarship.

Hornsby Shady / 30 - 1 / Age: 16
(Human Male - Thief)
Weapon of choice: Bo-shuriken throwing spikes
*Is 7-2 in amateur competition.
*Won the chest opining competition at Rettingham's Ambleinter Cathedral.
*No Thief has ever won the scholarship.

Mortimer Crier / 75 - 1 / Age: 16
(Human Male - Fighter)
Weapon of choice: War scythe pollaxe
*Is 8-1 in amateur competition.
*Will benefit from his senior year.
*Only loss came to a senior fighter in Rettingham.

Paganus / 100 - 1 / Age: 15
(Human Male - Fighter)
Weapon of choice: Buford stick
*Is 4-0 in amateur competition.
*Will benefit from more experience.
*His unconventional weapon raises concern.

Odds subject to change.

† CHAPTER 4 †

Dread flicked the betting slip. "You just asked an expert at the art of predicting this kind of stuff. I've been following the odds on the Skepp's tote board every day. Let me get you familiar with your competition. The odds makers basically have the Davi going to you, Tigress, Zombo or that worthless bastard Chaz."

My cousin loved to break down this stuff. I was already very familiar with my competition. Tigress, Chaz, and I all graduated from Beeston Abbey last year, with Zombo doing the same just days ago. I'd let Dread continue though. This should be good.

"Tigress is at eight-to-one. She got it bad because she's mixed, and although I appreciate her sexy half-elfness, the university don't. A non full-blood human has never won the scholarship, and I don't think that's ever going to change."

"But what about fighting skills?" I asked. "She annihilated all the girls she fought at the abbey. Her only losses came in archery competitions."

Dread shook his head. "It's a shame she didn't inherit an elf's good aim. A half-elf with questionable archery skills is not going to win."

"Tigress would have been better at archery if she didn't spend all her time breeding and training those sniffers. You know she and I were getting a little bit close during our senior year. She's like the one that got away." I sure missed being at the abbey with Tigress. Sitting in the cloister garden discussing fighting technique. She gave the best advice. I liked to think I gave good advice too, especially when I acted out some moves, but I learned more from her than she did me. Those were my favorite moments at the abbey.

Dread gave me the evil eye. "Tigress and her mother make a lot of gold selling those *highly coveted* sniffers. I would concentrate on what makes me gold too, and for her that's sniffer breeding. As for you two getting close, you remember what Uncle Riff said. She's off limits. Otherwise *I* would have got with her a long time ago."

A wistful expression crossed his face for a moment, then he returned to business-mode. "Zombo Packer is at four-to-one. Your friends over at Questing University have a thing for magic users, they've won two of the three Davis including the last one."

I had only known a few magic users in my life. Most could only do basic things like make water boil in an instant, or zap a fly dead with their touch. The lucky ones had deadly 'cave maze useful spell abilities'. The most sought after magic users, like Zombo, had at least one offensive, and one defensive cave maze useful spell in their arsenal.

By now, the square had emptied. All onlookers were probably at the stage. I should be there.

As if reading my thoughts, Dread ambled away from our shop in the direction of the stage. "Finally, we have your closest competition. Chazekial Manor is at three-to-one. Now Chaz has had a couple of losses against you at the abbey, but other than that he hasn't done anything to embarrass him self as a fighter. His parents own the meadery, which makes them the most prolific, and influential family in Beeston. Have you ever had a cup of the meadery's exquisite melomel style honey wine XO, Raff?"

"I've tried a lot of their meads. I can't say I've had that one."

Dread licked his lips. "Believe me when I tell you it's a fool. The wine pours dark red and has the taste of fresh raspberry, honey, and vanilla."

"How would you know?" I quirked an eyebrow. "XO meads cost

more than a bloated chest of gold from the Maze."

"I was lucky to be at the Skepp when a happy quester wanted to celebrate a lucrative run. He asked for a bottle of their best to share with everyone at the bar, the XO is what he got."

"Damn Dread, you making me thirsty. I'll be sure to invest some of my scholarship gold on purchasing a bottle." Before we'd even rounded the corner to the stage, the murmur of the crowd tickled my ears. Soon those murmurs might be cheers…for me.

"I wont be holding my breath, Raff. I bring the XO up because rumor has it Chaz's parents have been hand delivering free cases of the stuff to Chancellor Liberi, and other Sneinton residence who have say on the scholarship outcome. Also, Chaz's older brother Jeevesekial won this thing eight years ago. Jeeves has been a big part of the team's success over the last few years."

He nudges me with his elbow. "So what do you think of my expert analysis?"

"Do me, cousin," I said. "I want to hear your Raff Jenkins breakdown."

"Well you're the two-to-one unbeaten favorite, and beating Chaz head to head gives you an understandable edge over him with the odds makers. The only problem is that your father's got a past in Sneinton." Dread held one finger in the air and twirled it in a circle. "Uncle Riff gets around you know, and I love me some Uncle Riff for that."

I smacked down Dread's hand. "Just because he's a master of chivalry, don't believe everything you hear. That stuff about my father and Chancellor Liberi's wife is all nonsense."

Dread looked down at his smacked hand, then at me with a gleam of mischievousness. "Nonsense or not, rumors of your father messing around with peoples' wives, and countless other Sneinton socialites is going to play against you. Unfortunately haters have been known to play a roll in Davi decisions. You may also remember our fathers wiping out those non-hazard playing suckers at the old Sneinton gambling den. Don't think those losers forgot about that."

We reached the edge of the crowd. They pressed against each other, crushed against the base of the stage. Dust hung in the air from their movement, choking some chatterers, but not enough to quell the buzz of excitement.

A row of black robe wearing university students stood straight-faced across the back of the stage. Above their heads extended a banner: 'The Worshipful Company of Cave Maze Questing - In knowledge, there is gold.' A short, stocky man secured a podium front and center. He barked out orders to his flunkies, and then stepped back stage.

"My father's crooked reputation is going to be the death of me Dread," I said. "All that hustling has done nothing but bring our family's name down. I am going to be a legitimate questing professional once I get this scholarship."

Dread took a deep breath and exhaled slowly. "Cousin, my heart is with you, but my gold is on Chaz at the Skepp, and I hope today will be my big payday."

I snapped my head around to meet his gaze. "You bet *against* me, cousin?"

Dread slid the betting slip slowly into his pocket, and put a hand on my shoulder. "Don't take it hard Raff, when it comes to gambling I never let personal feelings get in the way of my paydays."

I shook his hand off. "You need a big payday after losing that death over-under wager earlier. By hook or by crook that scholarship is mine. If you put gold on Chaz to take it, then that's a losing proposition." I stomped into the crowd toward the stage. "Drinks on me after I win this."

"Drinks on me when Chaz wins it," Dread said.

A muscle-bound thief wearing a thick gold chain, and fine leather armor strutted across the stage. He tossed silver pennies into the crowd, and then flexed his biceps. Several young girls rushed the stage area in front of him. They waved their arms and screamed to gain his attention. One stretched her arm out far enough to grab, and pull on his ankle. He knelt down, took her hand, and kissed it before standing up straight to the right of the podium.

That quester got it. He had gold, women, fame, and adventure in his life...exactly what I wanted. Today was the day I'd get it too. Good-bye Beeston, hello Questing University.

Questing captain Saracen Babington took stiff steps onto the stage. He saluted the thief, pointed to a few members of the crowd, and took up a position to the left of the podium.

Zombo stood down at the stage's right side surrounded by several wide-eyed youngsters. He flicked his thumb to spark a burning flame on the tip. When the flame flared purple, then green, the kids oohed and ahhed. How weak was that? Most magic users could do that insignificant move from age six. Why were those kids so impressed?

"Let's get in closer Dread, we're too far back from the action." I didn't see Tigress there for the announcement. With the odds so far out of her favor, I couldn't blame her for not being there. I wish she came anyway. Once I won she would be the first person I thanked. Before my abbey duels she would always give me a rundown of my opponent, filling me in on their weaknesses. She had a great eye for such things, and often provided me with tips that helped me win.

We worked our way in about three rows from the front of the stage. I got bumped hard from behind.

"Well if is isn't the explosives boys." Chazekial took a few steps toward the stage then turned and looked me up and down. "Today I will win the Mondavi Scholarship, and join my brother Jeevesekial at Questing University. I do hope you have your gold bet on me at the Skeppers Pub, Dread."

Chaz looked up at the stage then back at us with a toothy grin. "I'm a lock for this boys. You should hope to be in consideration for the scholarship four years from now, Raff. I'll put in a bad word for you, or not."

Chaz cruised through the crowd to join his family members near the front of the stage. They had a roped off area with shade and plush seating.

"That guy's rotten to the core," I said.

Dread patted the pocket containing the betting slip. "That payday won't be rotten when he takes this scholarship."

Chancellor Liberi stepped up to the podium and cleared his throat. His cheeks hung low like a hound dog's and wrinkles interrupted any attempt at a facial expression. Old Geezer. "The prestigious scholarship I am about to award exists because of my school's greatest team captain, and this village's greatest quester. My friend Giovanni Mondavi died while questing in the Cave Maze fourteen years ago. Through his exploits, he left enough gold in the vaults of the university to assure that one resident of his hometown will be able to attend my school every four years. With Giovanni's help, what was once a training center for goldsmith guild security guards is now the top destination to learn Cave Maze questing. Graduates now make up nearly half of all accredited teams entering the Cave Maze. It is my pleasure to grant one of Beeston's residents a full scholarship to the greatest institution of Cave Maze questing mastery."

Jeevesekial stepped onto the stage with the scroll that contained the winner's name. He handed it to the Chancellor.

Chaz looked back at me and winked. 'That's my brother,' he mouthed.

My stomach churned. I'd waited four years for this scholarship. Four years. If only they'd offer it more often, but no… once every four years and that was it. Every time I picked up a sword this moment flashed in my head. The scroll, the cheers, standing here with Dread, all I needed now was to hear my name.

Dread bounced up and down and clapped his hands. "Ahhhh it's suki, suki time. Here comes the name of our winner."

† CHAPTER 5 †

Chancellor Liberi unrolled the scroll. "Zombo Packer!"

The crowd erupted in cheers. Not for me.

For Zombo.

Well-wishers swarmed him. Vixenett soared past me and landed a huge kiss on the winner's cheek.

"There goes wifey," Dread said.

I knelt down on one knee and put my head down. *That scholarship is mine and I did everything to deserve it. The odds makers had me as favorite for a damn good reason.*

I pick up a large jagged rock sitting near my knee. "I'm about to hurl this at that undeserved winner's forehead."

Dread shook his head and glared at the winner. "Oh my damn, another one. Magic users get all the love. One day the Davi will go to a real quester, a thief like me. We might as well face it Raff, magic users are in high demand with questing teams these days."

I stood, turned around, and pushed out of the crowd with the rock in hand. What were these people cheering for? Put me in a bout with Zombo and I would have my blade through his heart long before he could conjure up that stream of acidy slime. With no scholarship I was trapped in Beeston under the Jenkins reputation of low-life scum forever. And what was Vixenett doing kissing on Zombo? I thought we were dating. I guess I couldn't blame her. He was all but a quester now, and a magic user, and not a low-life Jenkins who lived in a rickety hovel.

Dread caught up and walked along side of me. "I should have known not to wager so much gold against a magic user. Now we're a real long way from the sack of huo-yao we need."

"We're not a real long way from the Skeppers Pub." I flung the rock into some nearby trees. "There's one thing I'm absolutely sure of right now cousin, and that is a whole lot of honey mead can help solve these problems for today. I need a drink."

"Or two, three, four, or more," Dread said. "Let's do this, I have an urgent need for mead."

The stomp of my footfalls felt good. Purposeful. As I listened to the rhythm, an idea sprouted. "Cousin, I have a back up plan, and it's an idea that's seriously going to mess you up." Oh, but it would *set* us up, too. "We *are* going to get the gold we need for that sack of huo-yao, melomel XO, gambling funds for you, and Questing University tuition for me. I'll meet you at the Skepp in a little bit, I got to speak with somebody before I break this genius idea down to you."

※ ※ ※

The Skeppers Pub was abuzz with chatter after the big events of the day. Dread leaned on the bar, enjoying—rather loudly—the company of two girls who sat next to him. They engaged in a boisterous back-and-forth debate. It'd only been a short while since I left Dread, but he already had a half-dozen empty cups in front of him.

I squeezed in next to my cousin. The bartender slid me my usual—a cup of Beeston's best honey mead. Our mead had a deep smoky golden color with entrancing greenish-yellow hues. I gave it a swirl to admire the way it coated a cup. The honeyed apple aroma took me back to good times here at the pub with the hints of citrus, aromatic herbs and ripe sweet fruit. Unable to wait any longer I took my mead completely to the head. It was sweet and strong with a slight burn that let you know it could take you exactly where you want to go.

"Nectar of the gods," I said. "Thorvald, another round for Dread and I please."

"It's about time you got here," Dread slurred. "I just schooled these ladies on how to wager and win. You know what cousin, I gots to commend you on the words you said earlier. They were so, so astute. You have never been more right about the fact that this mead right here can sure enough take away *all*, of your problems. You're my main man, Raff."

Thorvald slid me two more tumblers. "Dread, I got a plan to get rid of all our problems for real."

Dread hit his forehead down on the bar.

"No, really. Listen. We are going to put together Beeston's first accredited questing team. You, me, and some of this village's best talent on a run to take the Maze for some easy gold."

He squinted up at me. "You must be out your damn mind Raff. Beeston don't have the resources."

"I've done some checking. To be considered for official accreditation we need three fighters, a thief, a magic user, and a sniffer. After we get that we just have to pass an interview with the odds maker at Lais Dijon Tavern in Trosworth. We will then be listed on the tote board there where all can bet on the death over-under number the odds maker sets.

"It's a ridiculous idea Raff." He lifted his head just long enough to take a swig from the fresh mug. "I know the odds maker there, he would laugh the very idea of a team from Beeston right out of his tavern."

I sucked down all of my mead, sliding deeper into a place of blissful optimism. "There's gold to be made at this Dread, and I need gold for tuition, a lot of it. Accredited teams members making it back alive from the Maze are added to the quester-for-hire tote board in that tavern with one in-and-out mark. Once a quester is listed there they earn a minimum six gold coins per day when hired. The more in-and-outs, the higher your rank, and the more gold per day you make on the job."

"I got a job Raff." Dread gestured to the wall. "Look over at the

Skepps tote board. I have studied all twenty-six bets available on it, and identified three sure winners. My job is professional gambler."

"Gambler is not a stable profession," I said. "You're a brilliant thief, and I'm an amazing fighter. All we need is some slick recruiting of the right people, and our fathers' Cave Maze map. We'll make history cousin, Beeston's first accredited questing team."

A gambler near the Skeppers tote board laughed out loud and raised his mead up high. "Cheers to the magic user Zombo Packer! I knew he was going to win the scholarship!" The tote board moneychanger scooted the man three teetering stacks of gold coins for the winning wager.

Dread chuckled as he watched the gambler collect his gold. "First things first cousin. It surely takes a whole lot more gold than what we have to finance a questing team. If you don't have no one to invest, then I have no interest."

"I've already taken care of that. On the way down here I recruited Chaz. He will be our second fighter."

"Chaz? Really? I hate that guy."

"I'm not fond of him either, but he's one of the best fighters in town. He also has access to his family's meadery gold. We got a few conditions to deal with, but he's willing to finance the whole thing. He was just as disappointed as me about the scholarship outcome."

Another mead slid my way. I snatched it up and took a quick gulp. "Chaz was not going to stay here in this village tending bees while I'm off coming up with enrolment gold. He was hesitant at first, but when I told him about the map, he was all to the in."

Dread took an obnoxious slurp of mead. "There you go Raff. I sincerely hope you're not counting on our fathers' map for this. You know it's a myth right? Just the thought of a map that leads to 'a service entrance' meant to bring supplies into the Maze's creator is dumb."

I slammed my fist on the bar and the room went silent for a moment. I lowered my voice. "I got to see it once when I was little."

"Sure ya did."

I lean right up in his face. "I woke up one night because of some loud arguing. I peeked out of my room and watched our dads get into it about selling the map. Apparently my dad had a few questing captains in a bidding war for it. He had an offer of one thousand gold coins, but your dad didn't think that was enough. Uncle Mack went on and on about how unique and invaluable it was. He suggested that an entrance leading to an untapped area of the Maze should bring in a *minimum* of three thousand gold. I believe 'Packed with gold-filled chests', and 'guarded by little to no opposition' was what he said. If you know like I know, that sounds like a great place for us to start our cave maze questing career."

"You've been bamboozled." Dread actually looked sympathetic. "Let me tell you what that was actually all about. You heard them strategizing on how to pass off some *fraudulent* map for gold. It's an old quester's hustle that's been around for years. I'm not surprised they tried to pull it off. I see this all the time in the streets of Trosworth when I go to Moe's store. Beggars try to sell antiquated, or even straight up fake maps to questing tenderfoots. They'll almost always promise the map they're selling shows a ridiculously easy path to gold. Sounds familiar right? Raff our fathers are some hustlers. That whole service entrance map thing was just a part of their good game. You know how they do cousin."

"I know when those two are perpetrating a fraud," I said. "This was different. They argued over this map late into the night. Your dad ended up leaving the house upset, and with the map firmly in hand."

"Well that was a long time ago," Dread says calmly. "If they did have a map that valuable I'm sure it's been sold by now."

"I don't think so," I said. "As Uncle Mack walked out the door that night he said 'Riff, you can sell this map when you're able to unlock my cold dead fingers from around it'."

I grip Dread's arm, willing him to be sober and serious for a moment. "I need that map to be real Dread, it was my main selling point with Chaz. When I told him about the map his eyes lit up. He's in, and willing to finance this run, only if I can show him we have an authentic Cave Maze map, with a little known entrance. I need you to talk your father into letting us use it."

Dread slapped his palm onto the bar. "But there is no map!"

"Shhh, keep it on the low." I looked around and took a deep breath. "You know what? Enough about the map for now. Let me hit you with something I know you'll like. For our third fighter we're going to recruit my girl Tigress."

"Your girl Tigress?" Dread asked.

I leaned back and gave my chin a rub. "And you know that's right. She's deadly with those trident daggers, and has that bow and arrow in her arsenal too."

"Tigress *is* wicked with those daggers," Dread said. "But she sucks with that bow."

"Well she's a lot better than either of us. In addition to her fighting skills she doesn't go anywhere without her sniffer Mustela, and we need a sniffer to be accredited. Tigress, and Mustela will be a perfect match for our team. With them in all we'll need is a magic user to obtain official accredited status."

"And that's the bee in the honey bucket," Dread said. "Even if Chaz and Tigress are in, not having a magic user is an ugly problem. Without one user you're dead, raw festering meat in the Maze. Zombo is Beeston's only magic user, and after wining the scholarship he won't be joining us." Dread gulped down the last of his mead. "Thorvald my man! Another mead, quickly sir."

"*Actually*, there's another magic user in this pub, as we speak."

Dread tapped one finger down on the bar and looked around. "In *this pub*, as *we speak?*"

"Yes." I held back a grin. Dread would hardly believe our luck when I told him.

SKEETER'S HAND

⚔ CHAPTER 6 ⚔

Dread tilted his head to one side. "Who are you speaking of, Cousin?"

"We're going to recruit Skeeter. He's a Soothsayer-level magic user with well over twenty in-and-outs in the Maze. The man has even quested with Giovanni Mondavi himself. What more can you ask?"

Dread choked on his last swig. "Skeeter?" He cleared his throat. "The drunken fool that tells Cave Maze stories for meads? He hasn't been on a run for years."

"Well then he should come cheap," I said. "We just have to clean him up a bit. Let's go talk to the man."

Skeeter was in his usual spot, slumped over at a small table near the kitchen at the back of the pub. The brim of his brown leather hat flopped over his face.

"Skeeter!" I flipped a wooden chair around, plopped down, and crossed my arms over the back of it. "We need to obtain your services for a Cave Maze run. Dread and I are forming what is going to be Beeston's first accredited questing team, and we need you on it."

Skeeter did not bother to look up. "For a honey mead I can tell you what's happening up in that Maze."

"Thorvald!" I call to the bartender. "Can I get a mead for Skeeter over here?"

Dread sauntered over after me, seemingly reluctant, but I knew my cousin. He was curious.

A tall cup of mead was set down in front of Skeeter with his signature bamboo drinking straw already in it. He slowly raised his head and squinted our direction. "You two have a seat here now."

Skeeter maneuvered his lips over the straw and sucked half the mead down before coming up for air. "Let me ask you something. Have you ever wondered why I drink my mead with a straw? Have you ever noticed that old-time magic users always wear gloves?" He stretched a shaky hand out to me. "Take off my glove Raff, I'm going to show you what a real magic user's hands look like."

I pulled off Skeeter's glove. All five of his fingers looked like rotten dried up beef jerky.

Skeeter slammed his palm flat on the table. "A magic user's power resides in the fingers. As we cast a spell, one fingernail glows blue. If we cast the spell for too long the color will turn from blue to red and then burn like haggish gonorrhea. That sensation acts as a kind of warning for us to stop casting the magic. If you press a spell for too long that same finger will shrivel up, and the spell will either end, or another finger will start to shrivel."

I look away. I didn't know that about magic users. I didn't want to know that about magic users.

"Our ability to cast spells decreases with every finger shriveled. As fingers are lost, powers diminish. Once all your fingers are shriveled, all your magic is gone, forever."

"But wait,"-Dread snatched a dirty rag from a passing barmaid's tray and tossed it over the decrepit hand-"why wouldn't you just stop casting the spell as soon you get the red burn? And damn Skeet, can we get that glove back on? Looking at those things is making me sick."

Skeeter flipped the rag off his hand onto the floor. "My very powerful abilities as a magic user came early in life Dread. Those incompetent monks at the abbey didn't know what to do with it, and I wasn't going to listen to they mouth for three years. I jumped into

Cave Maze questing at fifteen as an off-the-board magic user for hire. Only unaccredited captains hire off the board, so I ended up working on teams made up of horribly unskilled questers. When they got into trouble, I would have to cast my spells for way too long. I saved a lot of lives, and lost a lot of fingers in the process. I could have stopped my spells at the red burn and saved my own self many times, but that's not me. I sacrifice fingers for my people. This is a trait you two won't find in magic users nowadays."

"That's why we need *you* for this run," I said. "Join us and represent for team Beeston."

Skeeter sucked down the last of his mead. "I lost nine fingers during my first year in the Maze. I went from a powerful four-spell Soothsayer, to a basic one-spell Magician. I did a whole lot for the teams that hired me during that year, but I didn't make a lot of gold. That's when being a product of Beeston saved me. The great Giovanni Mondavi himself hired me for his team, even though I only had one finger of spell power."

One finger? I scratched the back of my neck. This wasn't good.

"We quested it up something fierce in the Maze. After three years with Giovanni I earned my twentieth in-and-out, and Vavasseur ranking on the tote board in Trosworth. Unfortunately not even the best questing captains schemes always go right. Two runs after I became a Vavasseur, I lost my tenth finger. Now that all my fingers are shriveled up, I don't have magic powers no more."

"No magic power at all?" I asked.

"I can't even flick a flame," he said. "If you two are foolish enough to proceed with this you're going to have to hire a magic user in Trosworth for your team. When you interview make sure to check they bare hands. If all fingers are in tact, then they probably the selfish type that are not willing to give it all for there team. The last thing you want is a magic user who's afraid to lose a digit. They'll let you down at the worst possible moment."

Dread gently put Skeeter's glove back on his hand and looked toward the bar. "Thorvald! Another mead on me for my man Skeeter here."

Skeeter nodded his head and slumped back down into his usual position. Dread and I went back to our seats at the bar.

"So we don't have a magic user," I said. "I'm sure we can pick up a decent one in Trosworth, just like Skeeter said. And now we know what to look for."

Dread shook his head. "So the two of us, Chaz, Tigress, Mustela, and a magic user to be named later. That's the team. Enlighten me with the rest of your plan."

Dread hadn't given up on me yet, but he was about to if I didn't convince him quick. "Listen up cousin. My plan will have us back in Beeston with a sack of huo-yao in five days. This will give Uncle Mack one whole day to manufacturer the chest-busters for Joseph's order."

Dread dug deep in his hair trying to scratch his head. "A Cave Maze run in just five days? I don't see it."

"Tomorrow morning is day one." I tick off a finger. "We'll meet up with Chaz then go to Tigress's house to recruit her and Mustela. After securing them we'll be off to Chilwell where we stay the night. Day two we'll book early morning passage to Trosworth where we'll hire our magic user, apply for accreditation, purchase supplies, and get a good night's rest."

I hold up a third finger, trying hard not to imagine Skeeter's shriveled ones. "On day three we'll take the safe and easy Elfin Toll Road to the Entry Caves. Once there we'll utilize the map's service entrance to get in, snatch up all the gold we need, and get out. We'll make camp right there outside the Entry Cave. Day four we'll take the toll road back to Trosworth, purchase the sack of huo-yao, and stay the night. Day five we book passage back home. Not only will we be able to restock the shop with busters, but I will have plenty of gold for my freshman year tuition, and you can resume your gambling problem."

"It's not a problem when all you do is win," Dread said. "Does our financier know how much gold all that will cost? Booking passage and acquiring lodging for a questing team can get real expensive. Hiring a magic user and paying the elves' toll can soak up oodles of gold. Chazmiser and the whole Manor family are notoriously cheap. I don't think he'll be able to get enough gold to cover what it would take to make this happen."

"You just focus on getting the map from your father." I slapped him on the back. "Oh, and the chest-busters too. You said we have enough huo-yao left for three, so we need those made up tonight, at full strength. Let Uncle Mack know this run is going to get us more than enough gold for a fat sack of huo-yao, and that's going to keep the shop open for a long time. I'll handle the financials with Chaz in the morning."

Dread got off his seat, stood up tall, and raised his cup of mead. "Well bottoms up then! Like our fathers always said, "You got to make hustles bold, to fill your bags with gold." I'm in to make this happen."

Suddenly, the day didn't seem so dark. I stood and clanked my cup with his. "That's exactly what I am talking about, I'll drink to bags filled with gold all day long."

⚔ CHAPTER 7 ⚔

A stray bee buzzed by me in an early morning search for its hive. I passed up a few merchants pulling hand carts loaded with beeswax candles, jars of honey, and barrels of our signature mead.

Sweet-scented curlicues coming from the baker's shop called to me as I got closer in. Dread rested there on one knee, dressed in traveling garb with a full pack on his back. A young couple leaned over him, peering at something on the ground.

I stepped in closer for a better view. Dread fiddled with three identical walnut shells, placing a pea underneath one. A few of the couple's silver pennies lay in the dust for the winner.

A shell game.

Dread clumsily moved the shells around each other in a semi-confusing manner before offering them up.

The couple whispered in each other's ears and pointed at various shells. The man picked the shell in the middle, the obvious choice. Dread lifted the shell to reveal no pea.

The man turned red and clinched his fists. "But, but I—"

I did my best to keep a straight face but turned my head to hide the smirk. *Of course there is no pea under that shell. They don't stand a chance against Dread's trickery.*

The female companion nudged the man. "I knew that wasn't the correct shell, Soapy! What are you doing?"

Dread looked up at me and nodded his head slightly. "Hello Sir, would you like to take part in a game of chance?"

"All right. This game looks easy." I loved acting as a shill in this, the most basic swindle our fathers ever taught us. I tossed a gold coin on the ground and the game began. Once again Dread placed a pea under one of the three walnut shells and moved them around. I took a false moment then pointed to the obvious shell. Dread lifted it to reveal I won.

"Son of a leprosy-ridden whore!" Soapy screeched. He stomped away mumbling.

The lady friend gave chase, screaming and pushing him in the back. "How could you choose wrong? I told you, I told you!"

Dread flipped my gold coin back to me. "The shell game never gets old." He smiled and stuffed the couple's silver pennies in his pocket.

"You haven't lost your touch," I said. "But this is no time for petty hustles, please tell me you acquired that map."

"I got the busters," he said. "But no map. Turn's out *your* father has the map, or at least he should still have it."

I dropped my pack. "Not good." I couldn't believe this. Counting on my dad for anything but distress was bad business. He probably sold the map and spent the proceeds on mead, gambling, and loose women. "Chaz wanted to see the map before committing to the cause, this could be a deal breaker."

Dread put his hand on my shoulder. "Well you're in luck, Uncle Riff is doing his troubadour thing at King Head's in Chilwell for the next two days. Your plan has us arriving in Chilwell tonight. If he still has the map, we can get it from him there. You can also ask him why he is lagging on the huo-yao."

This just got better. My father's profession had done nothing but fuel the Jenkins reputation as scoundrels. As a traveling musician, it would be one thing if he performed in castles for kings, but he got down in seedy pubs and alehouses, hustling and womanizing all along the way. How wonderful I got to witness this first hand. When I enter the respected profession of being a quester, the shaky Jenkins reputation would finally be lifted off of me.

"Look," Dread said. "Here comes your boy Chaz now."

Chazekial walked down the road with a full complement of gear-a leather breastplate vest, high-calf boots, a stuffed shoulder-pack, and a beautifully crafted two-handed sword. It had a bright shine and looked fresh off the grinding wheel sharp.

Chaz set his gear on the ground. "Before we talk business I need to see that map."

Play it cool. I smiled and greeted him with open arms. "The map's in Chilwell with my father. We have to pick it up from him on our way to the Maze. I thought you knew, Chaz."

Chaz's nostrils flared. "Thought I knew nothing! It sure did not take long for this to get shady with the cousins, Jenkins. Raff I told you, my gold and I will not step *foot* out of Beeston until I see that map. I want to examine that secret entrance you told me about. You said the map is in your possession, so what's this stinking pile of rubbish all about?"

"No need for the hostilities Chaz," I said. "The map is in Jenkins family possession, we got to keep an item like that safe. We'll have it in hand shortly after we arrive in Chilwell this evening."

"That was not our deal." He swung his shoulder pack onto his back again, as if preparing to leave. "The deal was I get to see the map before we leave Beeston. If you two are changing things then I got a few changes also. Seventy percent of the Cave Maze take is going home with me, and that's *after* expenses."

Dread glared at Chaz. "Oh that won't happen! We got a map that leads to a honey hole. You lucky we letting you in on this run."

Chaz stretched out his two empty hands. "I don't see this honey hole map. You don't have the gold to finance a questing team and I do. No map, no gold, no Cave Maze run. The golden rule is in full effect here-he who has the gold makes the rules. I have the gold, what do you two have?"

I stepped in close to Chaz. "We got the map. It's in Chilwell. We also got huo-yao packed chest-busters, that's what we got." I stepped away and picked up my pack. "Tigress got the best sniffer in Broxington, and you got the financing. We're all bringing something to the table here Chaz, the Cave Maze take will be divided evenly between the four of us. You putting your gold up for expenses is temporary. You'll get all that back, right off the top, with the first chest Dread cracks open in the Maze."

Chaz slowly nodded his head. "Yes I will, I will take that directly off the top. Let's get on our way then, and there better not be no more surprises."

Chaz took the lead down the road toward Chilwell. I released a pent-up breath as Dread and I followed. If Chaz and his financing had pulled out, the run would have been over before it began.

"Hay Raff," Dread said under his breath. "If Tigress isn't willing to go on this run, would that be considered another surprise to your friend?"

"I got this all under control. Tigress will be in, the map will be there, and we'll be all good."

Our walk took us slowly out of the Beeston valley. The buzz of bees turned to songs of birds, and wind in the tall forest trees.

My father and I helped Tigress and her mom move from Beeston to their current home the day after we graduated from the abbey. It was a lot longer of a walk than I remembered. We made a left turn off the main road and continued down a narrow trail between trees.

Dread stood on one foot, held the other in his hands, and tried to massage it through his boot. "How much longer? My feet hurt."

I gave Dread a nudge, knocking him off balance. "We're almost there."

"Good," Chaz said. "Why anyone would want to live in the middle of nowhere I will never understand."

"I really want to thank you for being a part of this run Chaz," I said. "But I got to ask, why don't your parents just pay your tuition into Questing University?"

Chaz kicked a pinecone off the trail into the brush. "My mother and father want me to be a beekeeper and mead maker, but that's not what I want. I am going to be a great Questing University fighter, just like my brother."

"I can understand that," I said. "If my father pushed me to be a troubadour I would push back too. I plan on being a great quester, and a businessman. Once I start making gold from questing on the university's team, Dread and I will have the means to open up an explosives shop in Rettingham."

"That's right boy," Dread said. "I'm going to hire two of the finest young ladies from that city to work in the shop. Then I'm going to kick my feet up and manage the gold flow." Dread pointed through a clump of trees. "I think I see the house. And just in time too, my feet are absolutely killing me. It's my bunions, oh my bunions, they're on fire right about now."

"That is it, just across the stream." I veered off the main road to a smaller trail. "Follow me."

The stream was wide, shallow, and had greenish brown water that smelled of dead fish. When I stepped into it sticky green slush covered my boot. "Ugh, this water is way nasty. Watch your step."

Chaz trudged behind me. "I can't believe you two already have complaints. Your feet burn Dread? We have a lot of walking to do before we get to the Cave Maze. And Raff, if you think this stream is nasty, you will love the streams of bloody hell hound guts, and rancid orc limbs in the Cave Maze."

Dread took tall steps thru the muck, strands of slimy green vines hung off his boots with every step. "I'm surprised your feet don't hurt Chaz. With those bungling clod-hoppers you got on."

"These boots were made by the best cobbler in Sneinton," Chaz said. "The same man who makes boots for the university's questing team. Needless to say my feet are comfortable and have no bunions."

"Why don't Tigress have a bridge, anyway?" Dread reached the bank first and kicked a boot against a rock to clear it.

I didn't bother to kick the muck off my boots. It was too thick to knock free. "Why don't you ask her?"

"Raff!" Tigress waved at us from her porch. "Come quick, this way!"

She was tall with pointed ears. Her sleek brunette hair was in a high ponytail with two long braids running down the side. Her elven side resembled the beautiful coastal elves who lived on the ocean cliffs, not the toll-collecting elves from our light woods.

She ran into a ramshackle old barn alongside her house. I couldn't help but stare at the sway in her voluptuous hips-the tell-tale sign she was part human. Full blood elves just didn't have curves like that.

I covered my mouth and nose with my hands, took a few breaths, then raised my palms up. "Breath as fresh as an ice cold spearmint rhino! Let's go get our third fighter. Team Beeston is almost complete."

A large circular target hung on the barn. Arrows stuck from various places on the barn, but only one dangled off the bottom of the target.

"Look at that Dread," I said. "Tigress has been practicing her archery skills."

Dread laughed. "At least she was able to hit the broad side of the barn several times. The actual target is nearly untouched."

Chaz exhaled loud. "And this is going to be our archer?"

"You two know Tigress is a beast with her daggers," I said in her defense. "I could care less about her archery skills really, there won't be no need for them the way we are going to fight. Swords and daggers are going to do the job for us, we going to be a team that slices and dices."

The three of us walked into the barn. There was a large-scale open top maze here. Its vertical walls stretched high enough that a belette could not see over, even when standing on hind legs. A rope led from the center, to the rafters, where a system of thin walking boards led to a loft.

"The sniffer training area," I said. "Looks like fun."

Tigress and her mother had Mustela on an exam table in the back corner. Several small iron knifes, fleams, and tin cups hung on the wall behind them. A cabnet with various jars, and a cloth-covered glass bowl with swimming leeches sat nearby. Mustela was wound up in a spiral, releasing a low-whine.

Tigress dropped a canister of steaming towels in her rush to get them to the table. "She's preparing to give birth. Mustela is way to old to be pregnant. We're having a difficult time with it." She pinch-tossed several towels up to the table. "This will definitely be her last baby."

Mustela twitched, and rolled around in frantic convulsions. The whine now turned to a hi-pitched screech.

Tigress cradled Mustela's head in a blanket. "Here comes the baby!"

CHAPTER 8

The kit oozed out of Mustela's right ear. The new mother let out a series of rapid chattering chirps.

Dread backed away from the scene. "Oh my damn. Something just slimed out her ear."

"That's her baby fool." Tigress gently scooped up the newborn. "That's how sniffers give birth, right ear male, left ear female. We have a healthy baby boy here."

Chaz turned around, bent over, and heaved. "Disgusting! What twisted creature gives birth through the ear?"

"If you think that's unusual you should see how they conceive." She cleaned the baby with one of the hot towels.

"No thank you," Chaz scoffed. "Absolutely no need to see that."

Tigress handed the newborn to her mother, who then whisked it off to the house. She then fluffed up a pile of plush blankets and laid Mustela in the warming nest.

Tigress propped her hands on her hips, and raised an eyebrow. "So Raff, Dread, and Chazekial. I sure hope one of you brought me some of that good Beeston honey mead. We can celebrate Mustela's new baby, it's quite a miracle for a sniffer of her age to give birth successfully. Now if you're here to let me know who won the scholarship, I already heard. Zombo winning was no surprise to me. Magic users are incredible, have you seen the way he can make fire on his thumb?"

"Nobody care about that scholarship," Dread said. "Or that magic user."

"Let me handle this Dread," I said. "Tigress, we came here to talk business with you today, but I'm going to need a moment just to look at you. I sure have missed Beeston's sweetest honeybee. It's true what my dad says, you are the most beautiful girl ever to come out of our village—"

Tigress held up a hand. "Mustela has been in labor since before dawn Raff. You really need to let me get cleaned up before you talk all that mess."

I wasn't ready to stop the flattery. We needed her on our team and every woman—half-elf or not—liked a compliment. "You look great, midwife Tigress." I caught Dread rolling his eyes. "Sorry guys, I needed to get that out, I sure have missed this girl since—"

"Ahem!" Dread interrupted. "Raff is trying to say that we are here on some *real* serious business."

"That is correct," Chaz said. "Business, and I *did* bring some top shelf honey wine from my family's meadery. Lets talk about this over a drink, I am sure we can all use one after what we just witnessed here. I mean, you know, to celebrate the ear-birth."

As we approached the barn's exit Dread stopped where three chests lined the wall. The first one was a moderate pine box with two iron straps. He knocked on the top of it. "These are some choice chests."

"They have origins in the Cave Maze," Tigress said. "I use them for sniffer training."

Dread knelt down and gave the chest locking plate a once over. "It's just a simple pin tumbler lock. The goods in this chest would easily be had." He twisted, and pulled out one of the plate's fastener pins. "That is if you were clever enough to disengage this secret catch."

Dread walked over to the next chest-a large rectangular six-board design made from oak. Five iron bands and duel pad locks secured its lid. Decorative low-relief carving covered the front, including a precisely carved gothic inscription.

"Do you know what it says?" Dread asked.

Tigress blew dust from the carving. "It reads 'Remember thy last end, and thou shalt never sin' if I'm not mistaken. You don't want to open this one, there's a cursed amulet inside."

"Cursed amulet nothing," Dread said. "Watch how quick I open these locks—"

Tigress took a step back. "I'm told exposure to the amulet will litter your face with genital hag warts."

Dread froze, and then backed away. "Actually this chest doesn't interest me. What's the story with this other one?"

I stifled a laugh. Not sure if Tigress was joking or not, but the look on Dread's face wouldn't leave my mind any time soon.

The third in line was a large iron strong box with lifting handles at each end. A single bronze pad lock with a decorative figural cover protected it. The image was a male face with straight bangs, an exaggerated nose, and a vacant expression.

Chaz bent over to get a look at the lock. "An ugly face."

Dread knelt down next to him and lifted the locks cover. "The uglier the face, the deadlier the trap."

"I bet you can't figure it out." Tigress tossed her long hair back. I had trouble keeping my eyes on Dread's work.

Dread let the cover fall. "This is a trick lock. Any attempt to insert something into the keyhole would set off the trap." He dug into his pouch and pulled out a thin strip of metal. "The secret is the narrow slot at the top side of the head." He inserted the strip into the slot. "This lock is filled with a mixture of huo-yau and acid. If I do this wrong it's going to blow."

Chaz removed the shield from his pack, and held it forward. "What about the slot at the figure's neck?"

Dread moved his head in close to the lock. "That slots the decoy, I think." He gave the metal strip a gentle push with his thumb. The lock fell undone.

Tigress pushed the lock back closed. "The huo-yau and acid were removed long before I got this chest, but nice job Dread."

Chaz replaced his shield. "Can we get back to business? Training chests with no gold don't interest me."

Sure they didn't. But at least Chaz got to see Dread work. Chaz wouldn't back down from the quest *now*, and hopefully neither would Tigress.

"Lets get into the house," Tigress said. "I can't wait to hear what this real serious business is all about." We walked with Tigress to her front porch. "Come on in. Oh, wait. Leave those filthy boots out here, and next time find a better place to cross that grungy stream. It's going to take you all forever to clean those off."

We followed Tigress into the kitchen where we sat at an unsteady wooden round table. I broke down our Cave Maze plan over a meal of rye bread and stew.

"This was Mustela's last birth," Tigress said. "My mother and I will be needing a new way to bring gold into this house without her breeding. We've already taken a couple of advances on this baby, there won't be much profit remaining after we turn him over. I'm willing to join your team but there's a complication."

She paused and looked down with a blank expression. "I can't get Mustela into this so soon after her giving birth. Not only is she exhausted, but I should not remove her from the baby so soon. Can't we rent a sniffer in Trosworth, or just go in without one?"

"We absolutely must have a sniffer," I said. "Not only for accreditation, but a good sniffer will help keep us alive. You know that better than anyone."

"Renting won't work," Dread said. "No one rents sniffers to unknown questing teams."

"Right," Chaz said. "Even if we found someone willing to rent, the cost would be too high. We barley have enough gold in the budget to pay the elves' toll and hire a magic user."

I sopped up the last trace of stew with my bread and scarfed it down. "I've heard a lot of stories at the shop about successful runs in the Maze. All of them have included a good map, and a good sniffer. You got to have both or you're dead at any level. Mustela is legendary. Some of the best questing team captains seek out her offspring for their teams. We don't just have a good map, we have a great map, and with Mustela on the team, we will have a great sniffer. Everything will be in place for us to take home a pile of gold if we have those things."

Tigress laid her hands flat on the table and rapidly tapped her fingers. "If Mustela's ear recovers properly, I'm in. We should know her status in the morning."

"The morning will be too late," I said. "In order to stay on schedule we have to be in Chilwell by the end of today."

Tigress' brows edged together. "Well the answer is *no* then. Mustela needs to rest. I have seen these things take from one day, to a week to heal. I do know she will be amazing in the Maze. It's what she's been longing to do forever." She stood and gathered her dishes. "I got to go help Mom." She left the room.

Chaz squeezed his cup. "I will not stay in this desolate slum another night, much less several days. Having no sniffer is a change of plans that's taking me back to Beeston in the morning."

"We do have a time-sensitive schedule to keep," Dread said.

"We all do," Chaz said. "I had to anonymously borrow a substantial amount of gold coins from the meadery's coffer for this-a coffer that gets audited often."

I leaned into the table. "Tigress's mother is a wise woman, she will have Mustela ready by daybreak. Just let them do their thing." I leaned back. "We can use this time to discus our strategy anyway. I am thinking the three of us will make up the front fighting line, with Tigress and our magic user in the back."

"That's not how they do it," Chaz said. "My brother says the front fighting line should always be made up of the team's two best fighters, with whoever has the sniffer on their shoulder between them. That's where the sniffer is most effective at identifying danger."

I am pleasantly surprised at how much insight Chaz has on what to expect in the Maze. The information he's picked up from his brother's stories around the Manor family dinner table is invaluable.

Late in the evening Tigress came into the kitchen and took a seat. She folded her arms on the table, rested a cheek on them, and looked at me.

"How's Mustela?" I asked.

"Uggh, give me strength." She closed her eyes and snuggled in. "I'm going to need a tall cup of that honey wine Chaz, I'm afraid it doesn't look good at all. Mustela's really weak. My mother has resorted to an old remedy using vinegar and rose water."

That wasn't the news I wanted. I glanced at Chaz to gauge his reaction. He filled all our cups to the brim. "It's official, I'm heading back home."

Bam! Mustela pounced down in the center of the table from out of the rafters. She then swooped in on Tigress' cup of mead and lapped it up wildly.

"Hey Mustela!" I allowed my tension to whoosh out of me with the greeting. "Looks like that remedy worked." She turned from the cup, zipped over to me and licked my face. I stroked her silky smooth ginger and cream fur. "Congratulations on the baby buck, girl, very well done." She purred and rubbed her nose on my hand.

Dread tried to stand but stumbled and spilt some of his drink. "Well pour another round for Mustela and her kit then. It looks like the run is straight on!"

Our team's belette puffed out her tail, arched her back, bounced, flipped, and hopped around the house in a frenzy.

"That's the war dance," Tigress said. "She's ready."

I stood from the table to watch the show. "Team, we are off to Chilwell in the morning."

Several rounds of mead, and a lot of reminiscing later we prepared for bed. Tigress' mother made us up straw pallets to sleep on. They wouldn't have been very comfortable if it wasn't for the unusually nice sheets she somehow provided. Dread and Chaz quickly passed out under the heavy influence of wine. I was getting ready to lie down when Tigress quietly stepped into the room.

"Raff," she whispered. "I have something to show you, follow me."

I staggered into the door jamb, and wiped perspiration from my forehead. "That smooth mead really sneaks up on you."

Tigress took my hand and smiled. "You shouldn't drink so much if you can't hang." She tiptoed to a window that overlooked her porch. "Look down at your boots. Tell me what you see."

PORRIDGE

† CHAPTER 9 †

I peered out of the window and tried to focus. An old hob couple sat with Dread's and my boots in hand. The male had a long white beard and cone hat, the female silver hair and a lace-decorated bonnet. They both were extremely short, flat-faced humanoids with pointy ears and simple brown wool garments. The two of them smiled and bobbed their heads as they scrubbed and polished the boots vigorously.

Tigress put her hands on my shoulders and rose up on her toes. "Well, what do you see?"

I rubbed my eyes and put my forehead on the glass. A female sat on a box near the couple with one leg crossed over the other. She was slim, and taller then the others. *Is that an elf?*

She handed the male hob a canister of wax, in exchange for a bottle of oil. Her loose curly long tresses were the color of autumn leaves. Brown roots transitioned burgundy and then into glistening golden ends. Her outfit was the same color and material as the couple's, but a tight, low-cut version. *Who is this fine thing?*

"Either someone slipped a hallucinogen in my mead, or I see what I think are hobs cleaning our boots."

Tigress smiled brightly. "You see them? I knew you would. That's our brownie family."

"I've heard about brownies," I said. "But never thought I would see one, much less a whole family."

"Brownies can only be seen by saintly beings with extremely good hearts," Tigress said. "They're cleaning your boots because they know you and Dread are good people. They do small things around the house at night to help us out."

"There is something very different about the girl in there," I said. "Why is she so sexy? I mean she's really beautiful. You know she doesn't look much like the older ones at all. She could be mixed with elf, or maybe even human."

Tigress rolled her eyes. "She's definitely not full brownie, everyone can see her, and brownies don't get that tall, or dress like that. She seems a little promiscuous to me. What I do know is they don't like to be seen, so come on."

Tigress headed toward the kitchen. I took one last peek at the brownie family and got caught by the girl's gaze. To my surprise she smiled and gave me a flirty wink. I quickly ducked and followed Tigress with my heart pounding. That brownie girl sure had some pretty eyes.

In the kitchen Tigress poured a small cup of cream. "I always leave a little something for the brownies. Last year they scared off a piddling river imp breaking into the barn."

"I want to give them something too, for cleaning the boots." I pulled out my flask and poured a stream of golden liquid into a cup.

"Really Raff?" Tigress sneered.

"Just a little nip for the good brownie family," I said. "It can't hurt."

Tigress' eyes narrowed. "Lets get some sleep, I'll see you early in the morning."

I fell into a slight daze as I watched Tigress' sensual stroll down the hall. I had not noticed her curves quite like that before.

"Tigress," I whispered. "I am one hundred percent positive that lying alongside you, in your comfortable bed, will be way more cozy than that straw pallet. I'll sleep in your bed with you, but you got to promise not to grind on me."

Tigress smiled and gave me a shove back down the hall. "You need to show my mother's house some respect. Now take your drunk self to the guest room with all that noise."

I plopped down on my pallet and wrestled to find a good position. Three candles burnt low and dimly lit the room, I was already way too relaxed to get up and blow them out. A long stream of slob drained from Dread's wide-open mouth. Chaz bellowed out a slow bass-infused snore that was sure to keep me awake for a while. I gazed at the orange glowing ceiling and began to fade. My eyes grew heavy as I ran through our proposed Cave Maze strategy.

I couldn't have been asleep for long when I felt a soft, smooth, hot-blooded body crawl into bed with me. The candied smell of fresh roses filled the sheets. That mead must be really affecting Tigress. We'd always been close, and I often made playful advances, but this was a side of her I didn't know existed.

Hey, I wouldn't complain, though.

She massaged my shoulders and rode slowly up on me. Her hot tongue softly glided to my ear where she whispered. "Thank you for the mead, I hope you like the way we cleaned your boots."

I opened my eyes to see the brownie daughter from earlier looking down at me. She had amazing bedroom eyes that seamed to swirl in a memorizing whirlpool of hazel.

But…this wasn't what I expected. "Hey, um, it's all good. The boots we're really dirty, I appreciate you doing that."

"Do you appreciate me doing this?" She rolled her hips slowly grinding them into me. "You'll get no promises from *me* not to grind."

I gently put my hands on her waist. "Yes, yes I do appreciate you doing that. You are so fine, and got some nice moves too. What's your name?"

"Porridge is my name, and I need your help."

"For sure." Right about then, I'd help this sweet thing with anything she wanted. "But first tell me, how much of that mead did you drink?"

Porridge licked her lips. "All of it. My mother and father are more into cream. Will you help me? I am willing to do anything." She contorted her body into an S-form and shifted in slow circles.

I stopped her motion by holding her hips. "Slow down baby, you don't got to do all that. What kind of help do you need?"

"I overheard your plan to enter the Cave Maze through a service entrance. I need to ask a favor of you once you're in there."

The curtain that acted as a door to the room opened slightly, tiny footsteps pattered in the hall outside and low shadows moved.

"That would be my parents," Porridge hissed. She jumped up and stood along side my pallet. "I got to go, but I'll be in touch."

Porridge scurried out of the curtain.

This must be a dream.

The curtain rippled and Porridge peeked her head back in. She blew me a kiss with her glossy red lips then disappeared into the hallway.

I was sleeping like a log when my pallet began to shake. It then thrashed back and forth. I slammed my arms down to keep from falling off.

"You ready to get on the road cousin?" Dread stood above me, grinning like a maniac with a hang-over. How was he so…peppy after drinking so much last night? "I sure hope we get to see Uncle Riff do his music thing in Chilwell. It's been a long time since I've seen him play that lute, he's always the life and soul of the party."

I shoved his hands off the edge of the pallet and rolled back over. "It's way too early to start this walk, Dread. Wake me up when Tigress and Chaz are ready. I really can use some more time to sleep off all that drink."

Dread shook my pallet again. "Tigress and Chaz are ready. Spending the night here cost us a day off our schedule. We don't need any more delays. Let's go cousin."

"A one-day set back is not going to kill us," I said. "This just means an overnighter with Uncle Mack to manufacture the busters."

"Well one more set back like this and Joe is going to be at our necks. So getup!" Dread lifted up my pallet.

I rolled across the sheets and smacked down to the cold, hard floor. When I looked up Dread had all ready skirted out of the room. "I'm going to get you back after I get dressed!"

I stepped out onto Tigress' porch to assess the morning and tripped over a sticky dirt clod. I grabbed the rail just in time to save myself from a fall.

Chaz looked at me from his seat on the top step. "Excuse you." He dug a stick into grooves on the bottom of his boot, and flicked a chunk of slop my direction. Looked like Chaz didn't fit the bill as a 'saintly being with an extremely good heart.'

"Good morning Chaz." I picked up Dread's and my spotless boots and ducked back into the house. That brownie girl said her name was Porridge…or was it a dream? She said she needed help.

Dread sat next to me and held one boot up. "Tigress' mother sure did a fine job of cleaning our boots. Look at these, they like new."

I didn't bother correcting him, not with Chaz listening.

As we walked to Chilwell I forced my focus forward-to our run. I looked over the team. What would the odds maker in Trosworth think of us? What would our magic user be like? Would Mustela have all her senses working? Her nose should be fine, but what about her hearing? I looked for Mustela on Tigress' shoulder but she has disappeared.

"Where is our sniffer?" I asked.

Tigress lifted her hair to reveal Mustela asleep around the back of her neck. "Sniffers can sleep up to twenty hours a day if there is no action."

"Well there is sure to be action in Chilwell tonight," I said.

"Have you ever been there?" Tigress asked.

"I have," Chaz interrupted. "Chilwell is the halfway point between Rettingham and Trosworth. Questing teams stop there to live it up before risking their lives in the Maze, or party it up on their way home from a successful run. My family sells a lot of mead to the proprietor at the Inn there. He is a friend of mine."

"There it is!" Dread said. "King Heads Crooked Billet Inn. And just in the nick of time too, my bunions are flaring up again. I can't wait to get in there and have me a drink."

The sun was just starting to set behind our destination when it came into view. King Heads Inn was a large two-story stone building with a modest bell tower rising up from the middle. Attached to either side was a scary looking brothel, and large stable.

It sat at the entrance of Chilwell. I didn't bother to look at the rest of the town, despite my curiosity. Business. Everything from this point on was *business* until we returned with our chests of gold. Then we could celebrate and explore.

"I've heard a lot about the parties in this place," Dread said. "You can drink, gamble, and pick up a...uh..."

"And pick up a what Dread?" Tigress asked.

"And pick up a good night's rest," he finished. "The second level here has a few sleeping rooms." Dread elbowed me in the ribs and whispered in my ear. "I've heard the women in this place are wild and loose cousin."

For some reason, his comment just steered my mind back to Porridge. If only I could be certain it wasn't a dream. Would she be okay? I shook my head. Why was my focus so off this evening?

A beefy man opened the door. "Welcome to the Crooked Billet."

CHAPTER 10

We walked into a pub six times larger than the Skepp. The great room was alive with questers, mercenaries, locals, and prostitutes. They drank, gambled, and broke into spontaneous song. Several questing teams cliqued up in different areas of the room to swap Cave Maze lies.

Dread bounced past me and turned around. "Well I'm not disappointed. This is my kind of spot. Let's go take a load off."

We made a beeline to the bar and ordered a round of meads. Mustela happily trilled in Tigress' ear, then jumped down from her shoulder to the bar counter. She flipped, and hopped down the length of the bar, jumped off the end, and popped from table to table.

"Where's the sniffer going?" Chaz asked.

Tigress smiled. "Some of her old friends are at a table back there, she can't wait to see them."

"I got a few friends here too," Chaz said. "I will be back after I speak with the proprietor. He just might know if there are any inexpensive magic users in need of work around here."

Dread spun around on his barstool. "I really like this place. Look at Mustela, hanging out with various questing teams sniffers, just lapping up mead."

"Mustelas's not just 'hanging out, lapping up mead'," Tigress snapped. "After catching up with her friends she'll gather information about the Maze. Mustela's on the job right now."

Dread dug deep in his hair raking his scalp. "Understood Tigress. I'm just saying you don't see that every day."

Tigress whispered in my ear. "Look at that leprechaun setting next to you. I always thought they were short. He looks almost the size of a normal man."

The leprechaun extinguished his pipe, quaffed his ale, slid off his stool and stood looking at us red-eyed. He had a long beard and was smartly dressed with a brown leather coat, hat, and buckled shoes. "I am a fighter leprechaun, and a quester for hire young lady." His breath smelt like he was in the midst of a weeklong drinking spree.

He pulled a dagger from his belt and spun it in a circle with his fingers. "The little cobblers back in my homeland can't do this, nor can any quester in this inn."

I slapped two gold coins onto the bar. "I'll bet this young lady can spin a dagger faster than you." This hustle would be easy as a honey-stout tart.

With the dagger still spinning in one hand, the leprechaun flipped five gold coins onto the bar with the other. "I'll take that bet, but for five gold to be held by the server."

I matched the bet by adding three gold coins to the pile. "You're on," I say.

The bartender scooped up the gold and rang a bell. "We have a wagering opportunity here!"

Dread and several other questers gathered around making side bets. Tigress jumped off her stool, stood precisely in front of the challenger, and withdrew one of her triple bladed trident daggers.

The leprechaun began twirling his dagger faster, then pulled another from his belt with the other hand, and twirled it in sync. "Double daggers is the game, or there is no bet."

The corner of Tigress' mouth tightened on one side. She pulled her other trident and matched his rate of twirling speed.

A sour faced onlooker clapped his hands. "Well get on with it

Hooley. You're a leprechaun. Beat the girl all ready. Faster!"

The two of them sped up their twirling. The four daggers looked like mini hyper windmills, I even felt a slight breeze coming off of them. I'd seen Tigress twirl daggers many times before. Could she beat this oversauced quester?

The leprechaun's eyes glazed over as he looked into the blur of Tigress blades. He began swaying back and forth then stumbled. One dagger flew up into the ceiling and stuck. The other darted down piercing through his shoe.

"Aaargh!" Hooley hopped away on one foot.

The gathered crowd let out a collective gasp, then exchanged coins and departed with clamorous laughs and groans.

Tigress sheathed her blades and gave me a hug. "I still got it. Did you see that Raff?"

"Damn samurai Tigress," I said. "You are quick with those things." The server put the winning gold stack in front me, I took one off the top and gave it back. "For the tab."

"Thank you sir," he said. "Another round?"

"Yes! Another *two* rounds on me, and one for yourself."

Dread dumped thirty silver pennies onto the bar. "The next time I cook a goose, Tigress is doing the carving. That was impressive. I knew I should have bet more on you girl."

I pushed four gold coins to Tigress and pocketed the rest. "Looks like we all came up on that hustle."

Dread stared in the direction of a long table where a large group sat. He lowered his voice. "I want you all to see this. Look over at the long tables. That's questing Captain Castillo Gabbiano and his team. I've won a lot of gold betting the under on them. They're very good."

So that was our competition. Nothing we couldn't handle- especially with my old man's map.

Castillo stood up from his position at the head of the table. As he brought up his goblet, mead overflowed and splashed down on the table. "Bonnaroo, come over here!"

A stocky pot-bellied quester with a russet brown sniffer on his shoulder made his way to the captain's side.

Castillo took a pull of mead and wiped the froth with his sleeve. "This man has raised my spirits from ridiculous to sublime. He helped me acquire sweeter ill-gotten gains than the leprechaun king of Woodthorpe. Cheers to Bonnaroo Grifter, the best thief in all of Broxington! Les Trois Perdants will not elude us this time. This will be the run we take home the elusive chest of gold!"

The whole team jumped up and clanked cups with a rowdy cheer. Castillo then smacked a nearby barmaid hard on her backside. She slipped to the floor sending her beverage tray and drinks crashing across it.

Castillo pointed at the girl. "Bring us another round wench!" He then burst into laughter, his team followed suit.

What a bastard.

I started over to help the girl but got pushed aside by the beefy doorman. He stomped to Castillo's table. "Who's going to pay for these spilt drinks?" He roared.

"I think you know the answer to that," Castillo said. "I even got a tip for the slothful whore. Never pussyfoot on my drink order! That's my tip for that clumsy ogress!"

As the girl was whisked away by other servers, several large doormen converged on the scene. They escorted Castillo outside where back and forth shouting could be heard. If I'd been one of the doormen, there'd be a lot more than just shouting taking place.

Dread watched with a blank expression. "Les Trois Perdants," he mumbled. "I think I've heard of that. Hey look, here comes Uncle Riff!"

My father approached with a rapturous smile and arms wide open. He was lanky, and wore a three-cornered beaver fur hat cocked to the side. "Well if it isn't my nephew and my son." He grabbed Dread and I around our necks and gave a gripping hug. He let go and extended a hand to Tigress. She took it and he elegantly twirled her around. "Tigress. My favorite lady with an ermine. If you aren't the prettiest thing to come out of Beeston, I don't know what is. Why are you hanging out with these two toads?"

Tigress laughed and ran into Riff with a hug. "I'm going to let your son tell you all about that."

"Well tell me about it son," Riff said. "What's good?"

I took a deep breath. "The Mondavi Scholarship was handed out, and neither Tigress or I won. We're out of huo-yao at the shop, don't have the gold to buy more, and have a dept to pay Joseph Vega. Mustela is here too, she miraculously gave birth to her final kit yesterday. Now Tigress and her mom have no source of income. I know this all sounds bad, but we got a plan to make things good for all of us. Very good for all of us."

Chaz came back to the bar and shook my father's hand.

"Chaz." Riff raised an eyebrow. "You're here too? It's like all of Beeston came to see me play tonight."

Dread raised his cup. "I know I did!"

"Oh you're in for a treat nephew. I'm going to have them climbing the walls of this place. Now go on son, what's your plan to make all these bad things good?"

"Dad, you're looking at what is going to be Beeston's first accredited questing team, and we're on our way to the Cave Maze. Our plan is to enter the Maze utilizing the family map's service entrance, then skim the first few levels for gold."

Riff looked around. "Did you just say you'd be needing my map?"

"Yes I did, Dad. That map is the key to us pulling this off without getting killed."

Riff gave his goatee a long stroke. "We'll talk after I perform. I need a few drinks in my system to get loose for this show."

After inhaling six tall meads Riff disappeared into the crowd. He didn't seem too keen on giving us the map. *Don't sweat it.* He was my father...he owed it to me. And he knew it.

"This place is jam packed!" Dread said. "I'm glad we got these seats, it's standing room only in this bootch."

Two men took positions at either end of the small stage. The room rumbled when one started a drum roll on an animal skin covered, hollowed out tree trunk. The other man plucked the strings of a chitarrone so tall it nearly touched the ceiling. The bass line he produced created a groove that begged the crowd to move their feet.

The beefy door man came in the front door with Riff on his shoulders. My father broke into a furious rhythm on his lute, which sent many patrons, mainly the young girls, rushing to the center of the room where they danced. The beefy man brought Riff up through the middle of the room to the stage, where he jumped off and busted onto a body-moving melody. The trio transitioned to an upbeat drinking song that made all of King Heads erupt with drunken happiness.

The music was like a beacon to the connected brothel, it spilled half naked girls out onto the great room floor adding to the frenzy. I had the urge to order another drink but the bartender's workload had tripled. It seemed everyone wanted a drink in hand to celebrate the night. My dad waved for us to come closer to the stage. He then jumped down into the spirited crowd.

Dread launched out of his seat and bobbed his head with a neck-breaking bounce. "Riff sounds great!" He moved toward a redheaded beauty, grabbed her by the hand, and took her deep into the circle of drunken partygoers to dance.

I stood up and extended my hand toward Tigress. "Lets do this."

She drank back the last of her mead, took my hand, and pulled me toward the crowd. "You're lucky this is my song."

Tigress's dancing was as smooth as her knife-twirling. I spent half the time dancing and the other half admiring her moves.

After my father's performance, we returned to the bar.

"That felt great," Tigress said. "I see an open table in the back, lets go talk."

On the way to the table Mustela jumped on Tigress' shoulder and chirped in her ear. Tigress' face turned sour. When we took a seat she looked down with a frown. "Mustela's got word that the Maze has been a bloodbath lately. Many cruel new traps have mangled even veteran questers."

⚔ CHAPTER 11 ⚔

My father, Dread, and Chaz sat down at the table with us.

"Well Tigress,"-Riff wiped the sweat of his forehead with one hand and signaled for a drink with the other-"I can confirm that Mustela's information is true. It seems an anonymous questing team recently pulled one of Talhoffer's personal treasures from the caves. Whenever this happens the man gets malicious and switches up some things. New monsters, enhanced traps, and changing tunnels are a few of the twists you can expect. I've seen this happen before, it can be an ugly time for questers."

I grew nauseous. Going into the Maze with Talhoffer on the warpath seems wrong. Lives were at stake, and I, being the team captain, was responsible for their safety. Waiting until the Maze cooled off would be the smart decision here.

"Talhoffer's personal treasures are very valuable," Riff said. "Questing University's Chancellor Liberi has a standing offer of sixteen hundred gold coins to anyone who brings him one of those treasures."

Chaz practically fell out of his chair. He regained his composure, lifted his eyebrows, and leaned forward like an attentive pupil.

"Who's Talhoffer?" Tigress asked.

"Talhoffer is the wizard that created, and lives in the Maze." Riff eyed Chaz with a sneer. "I sure hope you don't think you'll find one of Talhoffer's personal items. It rarely happens. I was lucky enough to see the last one found."

His drink arrived and we all went silent until the barmaid walked away. Then my father continued. "A few years ago a questing team led by Morbosto Morribund brought one in to King Heads here. All Talhoffer's personal treasures are kept in fancy oak boxes bearing his crest. Morbo strutted in with the box. Everyone at the Inn gathered around when he opened it. Talhoffer's Gold Medallion rested inside. Wearing the medallion more than doubles a fighter's skill, strength, and stamina. After a long night of celebrating Morbo gave the oak box to King Head's proprietor in exchange for a bloated bar tab. You can see the box on the top shelf behind the bar now."

Tigress leaned forward with eyes wide open. "I was admiring that box earlier. It's exquisitely crafted. What treasure did this anonymous questing team find?"

"I haven't got word of that yet," Riff said. "I'm hoping it was Talhoffer's Hammer of Teleportation. I got fifteen gold coins bet that it is at the tavern in Trosworth. I'm sure it will be known soon, probably when the finder puts it up for sale."

"What other treasures are to be had, Riff?" Tigress asked.

"Let me tell you about a few of my favorites." Riff pulled a betting slip from his pocket.

Dread scooted his chair in close to Riff's. "Yeah, what other treasures are there?" He leaned in and squinted to view the slip.

Riff moved his hand shielding Dreads view. "The Platinum Flask of Basilisk Saliva would be a profitable find. A small drop of it can turn flesh to stone, or stone to flesh. My favorite Talhoffer item rumored to be in the Maze would be the Cane of Braggadocio. It gives the holder the gift of gab. I was told a zombie could charm the panties off a mermaid with that cane in hand."

Dread eyes widened. "We got to find that cane."

Tigress sat back in her chair. "It sure would be nice to find one of those items."

LAIS DIJON TAVERN FUTURES:
ODDS A TALHOFFER ITEM WILL BE FOUND BY NEXT HARVEST.

Blade Cusinart / 50 to 1
Diamond Incrusted Nostrum Goblet / 50 to 1
Platinum Flask of Basilisk Saliva / 50 to 1
Rod of Flame / 50 to 1
Cane of Braggadocio / 50 to 1
Hammer of Teleportation / 50 to 1
Gold Ring of Enhanced Wizardry / 150 to 1
Ointment of Metamorphosis / 500 to 1
Murasama Blade / 750 to 1
Werdna's Amulet / 2000 to 1
Mechanical Gold Cuckoo / 2000 to 1

Odds subject to change.

Riff smirked. "It wasn't very nice for Morbo. That medallion became a millstone around his neck. You see some of Talhoffer's treasures can be tricky. That medallion was a one-owner item. Once Morbo draped it around his neck, the medallion couldn't be removed, well at least not easily. In the case of Morbo the medallion *was* removed when a rival cut off his head for it. He would have been much better off if he kept it in the box and sold it. But it's like I told Chaz, don't count on finding one of these items. They're known to be located at least ten levels deep in the Maze, and usually under the protection of some unbeatable beast."

Instead of intimidating me, the idea of a Talhoffer treasure invigorated my adventurous side. I'd get a Talhoffer treasure someday-maybe not on this run but…someday.

"So what do you think of our strategy for this Uncle Riff?" Dread asked. "Do you think I'll be able to pop open the chests found on the first few levels?"

Riff chuckled. "Will you be able to pop them open? You're my brother's son right? Opining difficult treasure chests is a skill that runs in the family blood nephew. Chests on the upper levels will not be a problem for you."

Dread leaned back with his hands behind his head. "Listen to the man team. You got the best,"-he tapped a thumb on his own chest- "right here."

"Yes we do," I said.

"And what of the monsters on those levels Unk?" Dread asked. "Your son here seems to think he can handle hellhounds with ease."

"I never worry about hellhounds," Riff said. "It's those crotch masticators that put up a fight. They're just like hellhounds, but instead of trying to burn you up, they dead set on tearing your groin to shreds."

Dread grimaced. "We won't run into any of those on the first few levels will we?"

"Doubtful." Riff swallowed the dregs of his first cup of mead. "I would say you got to be six levels down before you have that displeasure." He looked over his shoulder, put one finger up, and motioned to the man behind the bar.

"Order one for me too Unk." Dread said quickly.

Riff threw two fingers up and shook them. "So you got the thief position filled perfectly with Dread here, let me speak to you three fighters. I've seen all of you in combat, and I know your skills. You won't have a problem with your foes down there if you follow my instructions exactly."

The barmaid set two cups of mead on the table. Riff and Dread simultaneously picked them up, clanked cups, and drank them down in one shot. "A quester with no instruction is headed for self destruction. Listen up close. First you got to pick up a decent magic user, look for one with a good defensive spell. Second is you must always take heed to Mustela's alerts."

Riff smiled and scratched our belette under her chin. "I know this sniffer right here, she got a nose for the truth. Now this last one is the most critical."

Riff adjusted himself, and then looked us over with stern eyes. "If I bless this team with my map, you all have got to follow the path that I am going to lay out with *no* variation. I will indicate five rooms on the first two levels that should have bountiful chests, and damn near nothing guarding them. If you don't find what you came for in these five rooms then you'll need to cut your losses and turn back. Staying on the first two levels, and knowing where you're at in the Maze, is the *only* way you will survive."

He leveled his gaze at Chaz, as if he knew Chaz's fickle personality was our weakest link. "If you start wandering off the path, or go deeper into this thing, you'll be biting off much more mutton than you can chew. You would need a lot more than three fighters to survive below level three. You know I'm not as worried about you all in the first couple levels of the Maze as I am about you making it to the service entrance alive. It can be a deadly journey just getting there."

"That will *not* be a problem," Chaz said. "I am going to pay for our safe passage to and from the Entry Caves utilizing the Elvin Toll Road."

"Well that is a problem," Riff said. "The service entrance isn't located any where near the over-quested Entry Caves. You won't be using the Elvin Toll Road, or the blood stained Trollbotten Path to get there. The service entrance has remained untapped because it is located far off the well-worn path, high up in the North East hills. You all will be traveling up the Carling Trail to the Ruins. That's where you'll enter the Cave Maze."

Chaz clinched his jaw. "Another change in plans, Raff? I did not agree to a journey up that archaic trail."

Did Chaz have *any* flexibility? I rolled my eyes. He wouldn't back down now, though. My father just admitted to having the map. It was as real as ever and that would be plenty to lasso Chaz's greed.

"Well the Carling Trail is the only way to the service entrance." Riff didn't seem concerned by Chaz's hesitance. "Chaz are you aware of how much gold the elves charge for the privilege of using their toll road? The cost has gone up to ten gold coins per head, and that's just one way."

"Ten gold coins per head you say?" Chaz looked away and scratched his chest. "The Carling Trail will be an acceptable detour."

My chest swelled. With every word, we drew closer to dominating the Maze. This was real. My dream and hopes were finally amounting to something. Soon, I'd be walking into the university with tuition paid in full.

Two half-clothed ladies decked in matching green apparel appeared on each side of Riff. One slipped something in his pocket and whispered in his ear. He calmly tweaked the tilt of his hat, stood up, and put his arms around them. "I have arranged for a couple of rooms. One for Tigress, and another for you three. You'll want to get a good night's rest. Dread, that means no gambling tonight. I suggest you all book passage on the first wagon to Trosworth."

Dread looked down at his boots. "Yes! The wagon sounds like a great idea. I'm through with all this walking everywhere. My feet can't take any more roasting."

"Come on up to my room son," Riff said. "I just might have a Cave Maze map for you to hold."

⸸ CHAPTER 12 ⸸

My father's party and I ascended a spiral staircase to the Inn's second level, and his room. Inside, two chairs and a small oval table formed a large sitting area. A window overlooking the woods at the rear of the inn let in moonlight.

One of the lady friends gently presented my father with a cylindrical brown leather tube, and then followed the other lady through a thick door curtain.

"You got a separate bedroom in here?" I asked.

Riff took a seat and laid the tube in his lap. "I always included the nicest accommodations available as part of my payment rider. This place is big on the amenities, but low on the pay."

I pulled out a chair and sat on the padded seat. "Thank you for getting us the rooms. It's sure going to be a lot nicer than sleeping in the common one with all those random questers."

"Enjoy it while you can son, accommodations get worse as you get closer to the Maze." He stared at me for a brief moment, then looked down at his hands and cracked his knuckles. "If you're going to lead a questing team into this thing, and use my map, you need to know the history of both. First let me tell you about this Cave Maze."

He laid the tube on the table. "Talhoffer played a major roll in the barbarian's defeat. He was known for his ability to mix crippling potions, magically infuse weapons, and design ingenious, magic-machine mongrel battle devices. After the barbarians were defeated he built a home high in the Hagridden Mountains with the intention of continuing his work in absolute peace. At the time his home could only be reached by negotiating a long twisty cave tunnel. Guards would guide his prestigious guests back and forth through it to his house."

Riff ran his hand across the tube. "Rumors surfaced that some of Talhoffer's gold, and magic items could be found in the tunnel. This caused treasure seekers to explore the caves with hopes of striking it rich. Some of them found themselves all the way to Talhoffer's residence. That made him furious."

"What did he do about it?" I itched to take the tube from him and peek inside.

"The wizard added levels and twists to the cave tunnel making it more difficult for strangers to end up at his home. But that was not enough, even with the new precautions uninvited guests kept showing up at Talhoffer's doorstep. One day a group of treasure seekers led by a Evon named Subooti made it to the compound and performed the ultimate insult… they stole one of the wizard's personal magic items. After that incident the party was over for good. The man moved a seedy orc horde into what is now called the Cave Maze, and went into seclusion."

Riff unbuckled the tube's top closure strap. "Talhoffer later had a change of heart. He had his guards post announcements stating that treasure would be dispensed throughout the Maze for those daring to enter. He even let it be known that a few of his magic items would be in it for the taking."

"So that's how the questing business got started." I breathed in the new information. Ah, the intoxication of knowledge. "Those first teams in must have come up on a lot of good stuff. The Maze must have been ripe for the picking back then." If only it were still like that.

Riff pulled the top closure from the tube reviling the upper portion of the map. "Not really, a lot of them died when they forgot everything that glitters isn't gold. It was quickly discovered that treasure seekers would not only have to deal with the inhospitable orcs that lived there, but also with a plethora of twisted magical, and mechanical killing traps he placed throughout the complex."

Riff began to pull the map from the tube but pushed it back in. What a tease. I almost laughed.

"Now let me tell you all about this map. Before the wizard went into seclusion he would hire your Uncle Mack and I to entertain at his parties—"

"Hold up Dad." I looked at him in a new light. "You performed for Talhoffer? I didn't know wizards liked to party. What was that like?"

"Talhoffer's parties were quite an affair. There was always plenty of well-prepared meat, fish, vegetables, and of course a bottomless cup of wine. I would do my thing on the lute, while your uncle amused with his conjuring, and juggling skills. We also had worked a revolving group of pretty young ladies into the act."

Riff smiled and raised his eyebrows. "Oooh, we had a fine stable of gold-making lovelies back then. Those girls really knew how to make the guests feel at ease. We were liked so much we got invited back to perform at all Talhoffer's parties. We got to entertain for some of the most brilliant people ever. The alchemist Paul of Taranto-or Geber as we called him-was my favorite. He would talk your ear off about manipulating metals. I'm sure he helped Talhoffer come up with some of the more gruesome traps in the Maze. I would also overhear discussions on philosophy, science, magic, and battle strategy. The possibility of a Evon invasion seemed a common topic amongst them. I was really upset when Talhoffer stopped having parties, those were Mack's and my greatest days as entertainers."

Finally, he removed the map from the tube. "We were given access to the service entrance during the Maze's construction. Guards would hide the way in by blindfolding us at first. But after they got to know us, and our girls, they did away with the blindfolds and took us through the service entrance with no obstructions." He carefully unrolled the map and laid it out. It was a perfect square sheet of vellum with black, red, and green ink. "This is side one, it shows the way to the entrance."

I stood from my chair and hovered over the table. "I knew the map was real."

Riff's head snapped up. He looked at me with one brow raised. "You thought it wasn't?"

I grinned. "A man can have his doubts, especially when it involves you and Uncle Mack."

Riff laughed and flipped the map over to reveal four equal squares in black ink. Three of the squares showed a labyrinth of branching zig-zag corridors, and rooms. "And this is side two, it shows—"

"The Cave Maze." The lines on the vellum weave in and out, patternless. I tried to follow one, but it turned into a different route that dead-ended. "Looks complicated." I started over.

Raff broke my focus with a snap of his fingers. "Feste the Fool couldn't have come up with a more confusing complex. Three levels are detailed here, one each per square. I will outline the routing needed to reach each of the five rooms I believe to have treasure."

"What's that in the fourth square?" I asked.

"Following this route completely will take you three levels deep before opening up to square four, it's a secluded basin surrounded by forest and hills. It's also where you'll find Talhoffer's compound."

"This map shows the way to Talhoffer's house? Where *did* you get this?"

"If they didn't want us to make a map, they should have never removed those blindfolds. It took Mack and I only a couple trips back and forth to produce this. He made me promise never to sell it."

"Way to go Uncle Mack." I looked closely at the fourth square. "What is the compound like? Did you get paid a lot for performing there?"

"It's not that impressive really, just a modest castle and small staff village with visitor lodging. Performing there made us a lot of gold, but the people were all too uppity for me. It was the after parties that made working for Talhoffer fun. After entertaining his guests, there was always a big grimy after party down in the staff village. Not only were Talhoffer's workers there, but all his prestigious guest's staff were there too. That is the place I found my original contact for huo-yao, it was one of Geber's employees I was drinking with at an after party."

"Where's that man at now?" I asked. "We could sure use some huo-yao. You haven't delivered for a long time."

"The last time I spoke with him he said the hags bought it all. He can't get any more."

So the delay wasn't my father's fault. "What would those hideous hags want with huo-yao anyways?"

"Son, I bet you didn't know that all hags are *not* ugly. Most hags are bluish-black she-devils that will suck the life out of any good man they can sink their snaggley teeth into. But every once and a while a hag is born looking like a beautiful human girl, they're known as succubi. Of course the hag community doesn't accept them, they lack many of an ugly hag's abilities in the area of magic. The succubi are kept around as servants to the ugglys. I know for a fact that succubi are sent into towns to purchase things for the hags. You might have sold some chest-busters to one or two at the shop."

"I don't think so. If a hag came into the shop I would know by her stank breath."

Raff leaned back in his chair, eyeing me with a smirk. "It's true a hag's breath smells like sweaty goblin ass, but a succubi's is minty fresh. I'm telling you son, you would not know the difference between a succubus and a regular human girl. The hags send many of their succubi to work for Talhoffer. They live in the staff village and do everything for the man from cooking and cleaning, to assisting with his work."

He looked at the bedrooms curtain and lowered his voice. "The girls down in that brothel don't have a thing on the succubi-they are some true seductresses."

"Please don't tell me you had a relationship with a hag Dad."

"Not a hag son, a succubus. After being oppressed by the ugglys they would really let loose at the Talhoffer after parties. I came to find out there is nothing haggish about them at all. I down low fell in love with a real fine one named Meridiana. She was one of the most beautiful girls I have ever laid my lucky eyes on. We would drink and dance all night long, then lie on the roof of Talhoffer's highest tower and drink some more. Mack and I would perform at Talhoffer's parties every sixty to ninety days, the gold we made was nice, but the best part of being there was hanging out with Meridiana. To this day she is the only girl whose loving was so good, she deserved an encore. Meridiana was your mother Raff."

Ugh! "What?" I reeled back, too shocked to stay focused on the map. "I'm mixed with *hag*?"

I knew the stories. Hags slipped out of their skin and into men's bodies while they slept. Once there they either pressed on your chest in an attempt to suffocate you, drove you insane with nightmares, or molested you to appropriate the species.

"Not hag,"-Riff rubbed a hand over his eyes-"*Succubus*. There's a big difference between the two. Your mother was no hag at all."

I put both hands on my head, leaned back, and looked up at the ceiling. *What am I?*

"I found out your mom was pregnant at one of the Tahoffer after parties. She wasn't drinking so I asked her what was wrong, that's when she told me. Sixty days later we came back to do another party and she was gone. The hags found out she had you, and took her back to their lair. They left you behind with the other succubi and instructions to turn you over to me."

I covered my eyes with one hand and blew out my cheeks. "Does this mean I have some of a hag's dark magic in me? If I'm half succubus, then I'm a fourth hag. Hags are magic users."

"I suppose you could have some," Riff said. "But don't worry, it would be dormant. Only a full blood hag could activate the magic in you, and you would have to let her. No one will ever know if you don't say anything, and you shouldn't. People are horribly afraid of anything hag."

No, really? Wasn't my reaction proof enough of that?

The bedroom curtain ruffled.

Riff stood up. "I got to work some things out with my guests in the other room, you take this map and come up on some gold. Remember, stick to the five rooms I indicated, and above all else protect Tigress. You don't want her getting captured by the orcs, they would do some obscene things to her."

All I could think was *hag, hag, hag*. I was part hag. And Dad acted as though it was no big deal.

Riff rolled up the map, put it into the tube, and dropped it in the middle of the table. "All the best questing captains have had their maps for many years and keep them closely guarded. I have known some volatile captains that would just as soon kill anyone who caught even a brief unauthorized glance of their coveted map. Don't show or tell a soul about what you got in this tube, they will kill you for it."

I sat speechless with my fists clenched, and head tilted down. I had rotten hag blood in my veins. And magic. Not magic I could use, but stagnant, vile hag magic.

"Son, I know this is a lot to digest, but you need to know these things. Weird circumstances come up in the Maze, and now you're ready for anything. I will be placing a large wager on questing captain Raff Jenkins and team Beeston as soon as it's up on the board."

I picked up the map, kicked my chair across the room, and opened the door. "Well don't bother checking the board for captain Raff Jenkins. I'm changing my last name to one that isn't hag-ridden, and can be respected." I slammed the door behind me.

Up in my room I tucked the map deeply in my pack, and flopped down onto the bed. The hag blood seemed to burn through my body. What would my team think if they knew their captain was partially made up of the coldest quester killer, and worst demon the Maze had to offer? If it got out that I had hag in me my career in the

Maze would be over.

Everybody hated hags.

Myself included.

I closed my eyes and put the pillow over my head. *What should my new last name be?*

PART TWO

"THE RUN"

⸸ CHAPTER 13 ⸸

C-l-a-n-g! The heavy bell on top of King Heads announced the morning. Four more clangs sent spine-wrenching shockwaves through our room.

I rolled out of bed and the first word to hit my brain was *hag*.

This is the last time I'll think it, I told myself. And that was that. Raff Jenkins-or whatever I'd switch my name to-hadn't changed. I was the same old me-a quester. A fighter. And, soon, I'd be a university student.

We joined several other questing teams at the stables taking various means of transportation into Trosworth.

Chaz stomped his way over to us. "I can't believe how much this ride is going to cost me, I mean *us*." He stepped heavily toward a mule drawn wagon and waved us over.

The wagon was made of semi-rotten wood, and had four slouched mules hitched up to it. One of them had several bald patches with fly-covered skin abrasions.

"Our wagon is the ugliest of the fleet," Tigress said. "And I think that mule has a skin condition."

"This whole setup must have come extra cheap," I said.

Dread danced a quick jig, froze, and pointed to his feet with both fingers. "I couldn't give a damn, I'll take anything over walking."

We climbed onto the wagon. There was a moderate seven-man questing team, and a few young mercenaries on board with us.

A few well-established questing teams, including Castillo Gabbiano's, flew out of Chilwell on horseback. Our wagon departed the stable at the same time as everyone else's, but took the rear, breathing in the dust of those in front. Soon, we were so far behind even the dust preceded us. Our ride bumped and rocked upwards trough the Light Woods. In the distance the towering Hagridden Mountains, home of the Cave Maze could be seen. Periodically, questing teams traveled in the opposite direction, their wagons filled with beat down questers sporting long unhappy faces.

The Maze is still being stingy with its bounty.

With the sun overhead our wagon came to a complete stop. One of our mules collapsed and convulsed. Dread, along with several of our wagon mates help drag him to the side of the road.

When the driver approached the animal, and unsheathed his sword, I positioned myself to shield Tigress from the pending euthanization. She sat intently sharpening her daggers using a fine-grained whetstone. "I'm not trying to see that," she said. "You know how I feel about animals."

Chaz stood to watch the proceedings. "Useless beast of burden."

I turned my head to check progress. The driver swung his sword to end the animal's misery. *Poor Patches*, I think. *With one less mule the ride is sure to be painstakingly slower than before.*

As we got back on our trek Dread was not seated with us. He instead sat with his fellow mule-dragging friends near the front of the wagon. *I hope he is gathering Cave Maze information, rather then hustling them.* I leaned on Tigress and rested my eyes.

"Raff, Raff wake up!" Dread side-stepped down the center of the wagon toward me. "I want you to meet somebody. This is Chugalug, a thief who's survived nine runs in the Maze. He's given me some good advice on the questing game."

Chugalug staggered over to us. He was an old soul with only one arm. The other one ended at the elbow, replaced by a carved ivory peg stump. He stood in front of me and quaffed what must be strong ale. The wagon lurched and hit a bump. Some of the emerald crystalline liquid in his cup splashed on my lap and the wagon floor.

Chugalug hiccupped. "This will be my tenth run in. When I come out I will be an official journeyman on William Ladbrokes' little tote board." He tried to stand tall but the bumpy ride hindered him. He peered at his questing captain and cleared his throat. "It's going to cost a lot of gold for this thief's talents when I reach the journeyman level!"

He lost his balance and plopped down into the seat between Tigress and me. "Hold my cup for a moment would you friend?"

Chugalug angled his elbow up and then unscrewed a cap built into the stump. He poured more of the bright green liquid from the stump to the cup I held.

"Brilliant." I said. "A very clever device."

Chaz turned his head and cringed. "Very *handy*. It is always a good idea to keep your wine at *arm's* reach."

"What is that drink?" I asked

"This enchanted elixir is called the Green Fairy," Chugalug said. "It's my muse, and not for the faint at heart." He smiled and winked at Tigress. "This concoction will give you the strength of a full-grown minotaur. You need to ask somebody about this drink right here." He threw his head back and swallowed down half. "Ahhhh, now that's the real mother's milk."

"So tell me Chugalug," Chaz asked. "Did you lose that arm in the Cave Maze, or on a drunken stupor?"

"Let me tell you what happened boy," Chugalug said. "I'm going to tell this story because I like your thief here, and it just may save his life. I found myself in a deep, moldy, stinking level of the Maze on a run. I had opened five chests with ease that day and had a bag full of gold. I was feeling real nice when I came across the chest that took my arm. It was ornate, and had Talhoffer's crest, so I knew there had to be something good in it."

He raised his eyebrows twice and took another swig of the Green Fairy. "I went to work on the lock right away and was able to open it quick."

That should have been his first sign, but I wasn't about to tell him. Any chest that could get open too quick was probably booby-trapped.

"The chest was half filled with crystal clear water. It had thirty or forty shinny gold coins at the bottom. I reached in to grab a handful when my team's sniffer pounced in the room screeching. The warning was too late."

He looked down at his stump, and then stared at Dread. "My body froze as a few dozen razor-tooth maggots materialized out the water and bored under my fingernails. They swarmed up my arm to my elbow when my questing captain acted fast. He sliced my arm off right there, keeping the maggots from getting into my body."

Chaz shook his head. "I got to *hand* it to you thief, that's quite a story."

Chugalug dropped his cup and grabbed Chaz by the throat. A pointy sharp spike sprung out from his stump, he lined it up between Chaz's eyes. "You need to kill the hand and arm jokes. Say another one and I'll stick my nub where the wind blows fowl. You'll doo doo nothing but elbow grease 'til winter."

"Chug!" his captain hollered. "Put that man down and come over here. It's time to show your fallen brothers some respect."

Chugalug let go of Chaz and joined his team. They knelt down silently and looked over the left side of the wagon. We rode alongside a wide unkempt field with several small broken tombstones.

I grabbed Chaz by his shoulders. "Chaz, we're trying to get helpful information on the Maze from these people, not upset them. You need to watch your mouth."

Dread laughed. "How's your neck Chazzy?"

Tigress tapped my shoulder. "Look at the Trosworth cemetery," she said flatly. "Not the place to be."

Chaz rubbed his neck, it was red from the wringing, and had scratches from Chug's jagged fingernails. "This is the perfect time for me to let you all know that burial expenses are *not* included in our finances."

I sat back down. "No one on this team will be checking into that bone yard. We got a solid plan, and it all starts once we get into Trosworth."

"Yes," Dread said. "Once we *finally* get into Trosworth. These cheap old mules are too damn slow. I can't wait to slide into that tavern. We can drink, gamble, and hire that magic user we need. I think they even have a doctor on the premises who can help straighten out Chaz's scraggled neck."

The other teams members bowed their heads. The captain did the same and led a prayer. "Thank you God for a safe trip thus far, and for the new friends we have made on this wagon. Please bless all of us here today with safety in our respective Cave Maze runs."

I thought all questing teams were made up of selfish, uncaring, black-hearted killers, but maybe I was wrong. Chug offered us up a story that he thought could save Dread's life, and not only did his captain take time to remember fallen members, but he prayed for the safety of us all. I gripped Tigress' hand, lowered my head, and joined them in prayer from a distance.

※ ※ ※

The wagon struggled down Trosworth's high road. Many bustling businesses lined each side here. We conveniently stopped directly in front of Lais Dijon Tavern, the longest building on the road.

Dread jumped off the wagon and stretched out his arms. "I finely get to strut into Trosworth as a bona fide quester! Come on team, let me show you around."

As I helped Tigress off the wagon a beady-eyed man on the road waved to me. "Got them weapons! Got them potions!" He limped over to us with his head down and opened a long coat. Several items hung in rows on display including daggers, charms, and talismans. "This is authentic Cave Maze survival gear. I got exclusive maps too, check it out."

Dread pushed Tigress and me in the tavern door. "Come on all ready."

Once inside, he lead the way. This was the biggest building I'd ever been in. One side had a pub with long tables and a few private booths. The other contained what they said was the largest gambling area in all of Broxington. Questers crowded both sides.

Dread turned around with a big smile. "This is not a loose party place like King Heads Inn, no prostitution here. This is a spot where serious questers and gamblers come together to do their worst."

Dread took a right turn into the gambler's side of the tavern. Five moneychangers had lines six patrons deep waiting to place bets. Several people played games of chance, including Hazard, but the biggest crowd stood studying the five tote boards that lined the back wall.

Dread stopped directly in front of the middle board, it was three times as big as the boards flanking it and ceiling-high. He held his arms out and looked it over from right-to-left. "This board contains odds and information on all questing teams entering the Maze."

A young boy rolled a ladder to the boards far right. He climbed to the midpoint and adjusted the over-under number on a listing. A mixed reaction of grumbling and applause could be heard throughout the room.

"Yeeeeaah! Ha, ha, ha!" A nearby gambler sputtered. He weaved through the crowd toward the moneychangers, looking back at the board all the while. "That's a bet Putnum! Don't change that number!"

I gazed at the board in awe. Soon team Beeston will have a slot up there. On the same board all the greats had been listed, including Giovanni Mondavi.

"Boards to the right show the current gold coins per day pay for all ranks," Dread said. "Boards to the left list accredited questers available to hire. One contains fighters and thieves, the other breaks down magic users. Rank, special skills, in-and-out marks, and several other pieces of information are listed for each quester. Now you will excuse me, I see a bet I need to make." Dread took two long-legged strides toward the moneychanger line.

I grabbed him by the back of his shirt. "Get back here cousin. We got time-sensitive business to deal with here. Let's go take a look at the available magic users' board."

"Fine." Dread hesitantly turned around and walked back to the board. "Feast your eyes on this team. From wizards, to magicians it looks like we have over sixty magic users to choose from."

"I like it," I said. "We should take a good look at the top twenty and start interviews."

Chaz looked over the board. "Do you see how much gold a top twenty magic user makes? We have bottom of the board finances, so let's just feast our eyes on the bottom of the board."

I examined the top of the board and my chest tightened. The magic users here were making six times the amount we estimated.

Chaz walked up close to the board and scrutinized the lower portion. "Raff are you seeing this? *All* these magic users are out of our financial reach. Even the ones at the bottom are several times more than what we agreed on. Looks like we will be going off the board for our hire."

A young smooth faced man slid in front of us. "Did I here you say off the board hire? I will run with your team for thirty gold coins per day, that's half the price of a magician. A real bargain."

We rounded on him. He didn't look promising—too…soft, as if a cold breeze would send him running back here for a spot by the hearth.

"What are your spells?" Tigress asked. "Were looking for someone with good defensive capabilities."

The man scratched his cheek. "Uhh, defense is overrated. Behold, the Ball of Bludgeon." He held out his palm. An apple-sized iron ball covered with spikes materialized and floated above it. "I can direct these deadly balls one after another at any enemy in my area. That is, if they don't run away at the mere sight of my magic."

Dread held his finger to the tip of one of the balls spikes.

"Don't touch that!" Said the man. "Er…the spikes are poison dipped. Very dangerous!"

Dread touched the tip. It poofed into what looked like a pink ball of fluffy cotton, and dropped down to the man's palm.

Dread pinched off a piece of fluff and put it in his mouth. "Fairy floss." He spat it to the floor. "And it's too sweet. This spun sugar won't hurt anything but my teeth. Keep it moving pseudo magic faker."

A wide-shouldered, well-dressed man approached us from behind the moneychanger area. He shooed the smooth-faced man away and stood tall looking at Dread. "Well if it isn't Dread Jenkins and Beeston's first questing team."

Dread shook the man's hand furiously. "William, my main man." He then turned to us. "I usually place a few bets here when I do business at Moe's store, William has had to pay me a lot of gold over the years."

"That I have." William looked about the age of my father, which hinted at experience and some know-how. Maybe he could point us to a magic user. "But now you're here in a different capacity. Introduce me to the team."

"No doubt," Dread said. "This is my cousin Raff, Chazekial, Tigress, and Mustela. Team, this is William Ladbroke, the tote board master here at the tavern."

Ladbroke. I knew that name-questers and gamblers talked about this man. He handled everything that had to do with the boards and gambling here in Trosworth, some said unfairly.

William took a couple steps back and looked us over. "A few questers came into the tavern from Chilwell this morning with word of your team's formation. I can't wait to post an over-under on Beeston's first questing team. Betters for sure will be lined up at the moneychangers to drop gold on you all. But first things first, I'm sure you're thirsty after that long ride, let me buy you all a round of drinks. I'll need some information to get your team accredited, and up on the tote board."

"A drink sounds wonderful," I said.

William waved his hand in the direction of the moneychangers. A barmaid soon lined five cups of ale up on the small bar table if front of us.

"What information do you need from us William?" I asked.

"You might be surprised that I already know a lot about all of you," he said. "You three are excellent fighters, and were the odds on favorites to win the Mondavi Scholarship. A lot of my patrons were very disappointed you didn't win that, Raff."

They weren't the only ones.

William fluffed the fur atop his full-length cloak. "I've known Dread's father Mack for a long time. He's a legendary thief. I'm sure the apple didn't fall far from the tree. And then there's the thing I'm very pleased about. Meeting your belette Mustela is a real treat. She has given birth to some of the best sniffers ever. I'm positive she'll do well for you in the Cave Maze. What I do need to know about is your map, and the obvious absence of a magic user on your team."

"We'll be going with the house map," I said quickly. "And hiring a magic user is our first order of business here."

"Ouch." William cringed. "Having a good map is always a problem with virgin questing teams. The house map is tried, true, and free but it won't take you anywhere gainful. There are much better maps available at the store, or even off the black-market.

"We will be good with the house map," I said "That, along with all the information we've gathered from questers coming through our shop in Beeston will do just fine."

William shrugged. "Well let me help you sum up the available magic users then. Have you had a chance to look over the board?"

I took a pull of my ale and focused on the bottom portion of the board, a familiar name jumped out at me. "Chawett Loinchop? I thought he was dead."

"Oh I get it," William said. "Chawett's from Beeston just like you all. He's not dead, and he's quite available too."

"I remember Chawett," Chaz said. "He is a Questing University flunky. Judging from his position on the tote board he is a Cave Maze flunky too."

"Well we know him," Dread said. "He just may give us the

Beeston family discount."

"I'll have my runner call on him." William waved in the direction of the boards. "Putnum! Get Chawett! Tell him he has a job offer."

William turned his attention back to us and lowered his voice. "I know he's your friend, and from your hometown and all, but Chawett is at the bottom of the board for good reason. I know a few top thirty magic users that would be interested in joining your team, I could arrange interviews."

"No need for that," Chaz interrupted. "The magic users on your board are not within our budget. If Chawett does not work for a discount we will have to go off the board for our magic user. I'm going to ask around about his reputation, and the availability of off the board help."

"Off the board, in the grave," William said smugly. "That's what they say. I'm not saying they're all bad, but there's usually a reason why they can't make it up on my board."

"Duly noted," Chaz said. "And I'm sure you don't get kick backs from any of these *recommended* questers on the boards do you? Like I said, I'm going to ask around."

I downed the remainder of my ale in one flowing gulp. "Sounds good Chaz. You just do that."

"I will." Chaz spun around and headed into the crowd.

Now that he was gone, I focused full attention on William. He was our ticket in with potential magic users. We couldn't risk this connection. "How long before Chawett gets here?"

"Let's give the man some time to get presentable," William said. "I'll have him meet you on the pub side in a while. One more question, are you the one I am going to be listing as team captain, Raff?"

"Yes, but I don't want to be listed as Raff Jenkins. I want to change my last name."

"That's a bit unusual," William said. "I guess we all got things to hide. What's it going to be? Captain Raff what?"

MOE'S SCALE

⚔ CHAPTER 14 ⚔

"Orcslaughter!" It took a full mule-ride and a head-scratch to think up that last name.

"Really Raff?" Dread said. "Orcslaughter?"

"I'm not going to let the Jenkins name do anything to bring this team down," I said.

"Consider it done Mr. Orcslaughter," William said.

I swallowed down my ale. "Thanks for the snort, William. We're going next-door to the store, we'll be back to rectify the magic user situation later."

The provisions store had a small front with a door in the center, and two square windows at either side. Once in we found the building was narrow, extremely long, and cluttered with questing equipment. A jovial bald man approached. "Dread! Good to see you. I sure hope you're here to sell me some more chest-busters. I'm willing to pay you three times the gold I paid for my last order."

"Not this time Moe," Dread said. "What I need is some huo-yao to *make* more chest-busters."

"I may be able to help you with that," Moe said. "I should have a couple of sacks on my shelf in the next few days. I'll be selling them for three hundred and fifty gold coins each if you are interested."

"Three fifty?" Dread gasps.

Moe went back behind the counter. "It's a crazy high price right. The hags continue to drive it up that way, they'll pay three hundred fifty gold all day long."

"Why do they want it so bad?" Dread asked.

"The hags give the powder to Talhoffer. They will do anything for that man and his experiments. Huo-yao has become extremely hard to come by Dread, once these sacks are gone I don't think I'll see anymore for a long time."

"I got a deal for you Moe," Dread said. "Hold one sack for me until I get back from this run in the Maze. Do that, and not only will I pay your asking price, but I'll also give you first crack at buying the chest-busters we make from it."

Moe moaned. "Can't do it, not with huo-yao. Give me a fifty percent deposit. That's what it is going to take for me to hold it for you."

Dread set a sack on the counter. "We can put a third down. There's one hundred and ten gold coins in here."

It hurt me to see that sack in play. Besides what little I had in my pocket, that was all the gold we got.

Moe sat the sack on the tray of a balance scale and snapped his fingers. Three oversized golden grasshoppers jumped in the other tray. Moe watched them balance and nodded his head.

Tigress wiggled her finger near the grasshoppers. "Cute, they look like real gold."

"They're partially mechanical," Moe said. "Possibly a Talhoffer creation. They're also excellent moneychangers. If the weight of this gold was off, or the coins counterfeit, they would know."

One of the grasshoppers went to the edge of the tray, looked up at Tigress and rubbed its hind leg. A melodic chirp filled the room.

"Stop flirting Gresham." Moe swished his hand causing the grasshoppers to scatter. "I'm trying to conduct business here." He eyeballed the sack. "This is okay Dread. Your price is locked in, but no refunds."

"All good Moe," Dread said. "What we need now is some supplies for this run."

"I was told you're part of a new questing team early today," Moe said.

Dread dug into his hair and gave his head a hearty scratch. "Word gets around these parts fast. This is Tigress, Mustela, and my cousin Raff. We're going in tomorrow morning."

Moe looked at us and nodded. "I have some great potions in stock that could really help your team be a success in the Maze, guaranteed." He pointed behind him to a row of clear glass bottles filled with colored liquids. "Drink this pink one and your spit will paralyze anything it touches for half a day. This black and tan potion will quadruple an archer's aim and arm strength for a full day."

Too bad all our gold sat in the sack on his scales.

Dread elbowed Tigress. "There you go girl, that black and tan one there. That's exactly what you need."

Tigress rolled her eyes. "What's with those?" She pointed to the highest shelf behind Moe. "The bottles with moving pictures in the liquid. That sky blue one is beautiful."

Moe smiled at the potions. "Those are potions of teleportation. They are very expensive but well worth it. Drink one, and you get transported to the place pictured live in the bottle. That blue one you're looking at is extremely rare. It will take you all the way to the Ambleinter Cathedral in Rettingham. The priests at the cathedral are very good at curing spells cast by the undead. This is a great potion if you're making a run in the northwest area of the Maze. Take a look at this one young lady, it's very popular amongst questers, we have plenty, and I can make the price right for you."

Moe handed Tigress a triangle shaped glass bottle. There was a large dark cave surrounded by waving trees pictured in the light green liquid. A group of questers could be seen entering the cave.

"That's a live picture of the main entry cave to the Maze," Moe said. "Drink this potion and you will be there instantly. No need to pay the elves for the privilege of using their toll road, or risk your life traveling the Trollebotten path."

Tigress stared into the glass. "It's amazing, where do you get these?"

Moe wiggled the potion from Tigress' hand and placed it back on the shelf. "Most of them come in from questers. They find many unique and valuable things in that Maze. Then they sell them to me for gold or trade. I don't ask questions."

Tigress pointed toward a rooster in a square handled wooden cage. There were several of them, big and small. "Why do you sell these roosters, what do they have to do with questing?"

Moe picked up a crudely framed mirror from a stack at his counter. "I sell roosters for the same reason I sell these mirrors, you never know when you'll run into a Rex."

"What's a Rex?" Tigress asked.

"Rex Goliath is the most vicious, and ill-tempered of all the cockatrice," Moe said.

Tigress poked a seed coated stick into the rooster's cage. "And what's a cockatrice?"

"Cockatrice are not much unlike a rooster," Moe said. "They have the head, torso and legs of a cock, but then it gets perverse. They have the tongue and tail of a serpent, and the wings of a bat. The creatures sparsely inhabit the Thorneywood Forest up and down the Trollebotten River, but wander here into Trosworth from time to time."

He took our sack of gold off the scales and tucked it into his belt. "If you run into one beware, they have a poisonous bite, and their glance will turn you to stone. The people who live around here like to keep roosters as pets because their call means instant death to a cockatrice. Questers like to keep mirrors because they are a safe way to view a cock. Mirrors can also be used to deflect their glance back at them, turning them into stone. But you don't have to worry about the cockatrice miss."

Tigress pulled the now bare stick from the cage. "Why is that?"

"Because you have a fine looking sniffer on your shoulder. Sniffers are the passionate natural enemy of the cockatrice, they're immune to their gaze and poisons. If a cock comes around you'll know by the reaction of your sniffer. She'll go crazy with rage."

Dread laid two torches and a flask of oil on the counter. "We won't be needing any of your potions Moe. And thanks to Mustela here, we won't need a rooster or mirrors. This is all for today."

Moe walked us outside of his store. "You all need to watch yourselves in the Maze, that thing is scorching hot right now. Take a look over there."

Two bloodied men helped a shredded up man along the high road. Four others staggered behind them.

"No celebrating," Moe said. "No flaunting of treasure. That team left town with a dozen men, they come back with…seven."

"Where are they going?" Tigress asked.

Moe pulled a wadded betting slip from his pocket and tried his best to straighten it. "They're headed to the church for healing. And to register their dead."

Dread peeked at Moe's slip. "Good thing you bet the under on them."

Moe smiled and folded the slip into a neat, sharp square. "Yes it is! The under has been a good friend of mine lately."

A bit morbid, but that was how the Maze-game worked. Sometimes, a handful of deaths worked in one's favor.

We walked back over to Lais Dijon Tavern. The tote board area was jam packed with excited patrons pushing and shoving each other to get in line at the moneychangers.

"What's going on in the pit Dread?" I asked.

"That much commotion can only be created by one thing," he said. "There must be a newly posted over-under. Judging by the amount of action being taken it's probably Castillo's team they're betting on. We should get in on this—"

I held my arm up to block Dread's way. "Hold up cousin. You know we're not here for all that. We got a meeting on the other side."

The pub area was standing room only. Team members, captains, and mercenaries jammed the place with boisterous questing conversation. Castillo Gabbiano and his team sat at one of the long tables having a gluttonous pre-quest meal.

"Team Beeston!" William said. "I got a private booth waiting for you all. Your friend Chawett is already there. Just go around the bar to the back, you'll see him."

Chawett stood to greet us from the booth. His clothes had holes in them, and he looked a lot heavier than before. He still wore the slumped cone hat that I remembered, only now it had a few ostrich feathers protruding from one side.

"Chawett." I said. "Good to see you again—"

Dread cut in front of me and extended his hand. "The king of the lava sphere! Chawett Loinchop, my man!"

The magic user did not return Dread's handshake. He just stared at us. "If this conversation isn't going to make me a huge pile of gold, then I don't know why you're talking to me right now."

⚔ CHAPTER 15 ⚔

"Whoa," I froze in my steps. "Did William let you know of our situation?"

Chawett sat down and twisted in the seat. "He did, and I appreciate the opportunity to be part of Beeston's first questing team. You must have noticed that I am ranked as a soothsayer on the magic user tote board."

Chaz came over and took a seat. "You're ranked last, Chawett. *Dead* last. And what kind of soothsayer gets ranked behind conjurers and even magicians? Word around the tavern is your spells stop working prematurely, and in the heat of battle."

Tigress, Dread, and I took seats around the table. I peered at Chawett's hands, but he dropped them out of sight, into his lap. Not before I saw them, though. "With a bad reputation, and low ranking, you won't see that huge pile of gold. I noticed all your fingers are intact. They're actually really well manicured. Tell me, are you willing to get your fingers dirty?"

"Watch this." Chawett slightly raised his hand. "Keep your eye on Captain Gabbiano's meal." He pointed one finger at the giant mutton shank on Castillo's plate. It elevated along with his finger.

Tigress gave me a nudge and whispered in my ear. "Look at the nail on Chawett's finger, it's glowing. What he's doing is amazing."

Chawett twitched his hand. Castillo's greasy mutton shank dropped off the table and splattered directly on a burley passerby's boot. The man stopped, looked down at his slatternly boot, and glared at Castillo. He then gave a thrusting kick sending the sloppy shank flying across the room. It slapped into the side of an unsuspecting man's face, knocking him off his feet to the floor.

Dread howled and slapped his hand on the table. "Now that was some great magic right there!"

Tigress had tears in her eyes from laughter. She covered her mouth and ducked behind Dread's shoulder.

Castillo reached for his dinner to find it gone. He looked around confused then grabbed another shank.

Chawett leaned into the table and lowered his voice. "Lookit here, Castillo hired me on a failed quest a while back. I signed on for a five-day run that ended up going ten days. I can cast magic great on short runs, for long runs not so good. My lava sphere fizzled at a bad time on the seventh day and some men were lost. Castillo's all but had me blackballed ever since. As for the appearance of my fingers, I'm not willing to get them dirty for you, William, Castillo, or anyone else. Dirty fingers equals less magic in the soul. I don't do less magic partner."

"All good Chawett," I said. "We're planning on a short, three day run with just one day in the actual Maze. We're not even going more than a few levels deep. This opportunity is a perfect match for you family."

Chaz gruffly cleared his throat. "A perfect match at a *big* blackballed discount of course."

Chawett leaned back slowly and sunk into his chair. "A successful run in the Maze will do a lot to restore my name up on the tote board. I'm only one in-and-out away from the journeyman level, so your run does interest me."

This sounded better and better.

"The problem is I don't play that discount nonsense. Blackballed or not, I'm a ranked magic user for a reason. I can help you Cave Maze tenderfoots stay alive. Now considering that we all have

Beeston lineage, I am willing to work with you. The current minimum for a ranked magic user is sixty gold coins per day, plus in-and-out pay. I'll do you the favor of settling for that, but I want ten percent of the spoils too. We *are* home town family after all."

Chaz shook his head. "Oh no! There is no way I'll pay that much to a reject. We'll be going off the board for our magic user thank you."

I didn't like how quick Chaz chose to back out of an option. Had he never heard of bargaining?

Chawett chuckled. "Off the board, in the grave. Some of these mercenaries will set you up to get robbed, or will desert you as soon as they smell the stench of an orc's breath. Do your best off the board Chaz, you won't live to regret it."

"Hold up my man," Dread said. "We have a map that's going to make this run easier than a Cock's Lane wench. Believe me Chawett, you want a piece of this."

Chawett ran two fingers along his hats ostrich feathers. "William told me your team is working with the house map. The house map doesn't do a damn thing to make me want a piece of what you're doing, Dread."

I bit my lip trying not to reveal the truth about our map. Going off the board meant we could end up with a no-good, fairy floss magic user like we met earlier. Chawett was accredited, and we knew his magic was legit. I needed to make this happen for the safety of the team, and the success of our run.

I went for it. "Well in actuality we'll be using a map Dread and I got from our fathers. It's not a common entrance we're going to use. You know better than I do not to make that public to William…or anyone else for that matter."

"Now *that* might make a difference," Chawett said. "A run that utilizes a map from Riff and Mack Jenkins does pique my interest. I've heard some implausible stories of your fathers' Cave Maze endeavors."

Dread elbowed me. "See that cousin? The Jenkins name got pull."

I waved Dread off. "So you know this opportunity is good business then Chawett."

"Can't do it." The magic user rocked back and forth in his chair. "I get paid board plus ten or I'm out."

"How about this," I said. "Lets do one-fifth of the take after total expenses. We'll go in as a true questing team, splitting the profit even amongst the five of us."

Chawett stared at me for a moment. "You can count me in with the even gold split."

"Ah-ha!" I wiped sweat from my forehead. "We've got what is soon to be an accredited questing team then." We all stood and shook hands.

Tigress gave Chawett a hug. "Can you tell me how you did that thing with the mutton shank? What spell was that?"

"I call it floating fair." He beamed up at her, soaking in her attention. Admittedly, a twinge of jealousy hit my gut. "That spell gives me the ability to levitate and move all types of meat. I can conjure up that nonsense at full power over ten times in a three-day span. If you don't know that's at the wizard level of proficiency. Unfortunately floating fair is not considered a Cave Maze useful spell, so I don't get no love for it."

"How did you get so good at such an oddball spell?" I asked.

"I come from a family of butchers," Chawett said. "I started to build strength with that spell when I was young to help my family with the business. My father encouraged my power over meat and was grooming me to be the best butcher in Broxington. I didn't want to be a butcher, I wanted to be a quester, so I had to run away in order to learn Cave Maze useful spells. That's why you won't see me back in Beeston, my father will never forgive me for that move."

Chaz rolled his eyes and chuckled. "Very impressive, if we get into a Cave Maze food fight that floating meat thing you do will come in useful." His playfulness died and he leaned both hands on the table. "Let me make sure you understand this contract Chawett. We will split one-fifth of the total take *after* expenses, and the expenses have been adding up quick."

I pulled Chaz back. "The man's a professional, Chaz, he understands what after expenses means."

Chaz hesitantly put three keys in my hand. "Speaking of expenses here are your room keys. I had my eye on a pile of hay in the stable, but William was kind enough to arrange discounted rooms for each of us at his Inn."

"Nice." I handed keys to Dread and Tigress. "I've heard good things about the Questers Inn. I'm sure we can all use some rest, let's meet up here early in the morning."

Dread dropped the room key in his pocket, clapped his hands, and smiled. "You aren't my daddy Raff. There's no way I'm going to sleep until I see our team listed up on that tote board. I'm going to find William and inform him our lineup is complete. Chawett, let's catch up over an ale my man, I'm in the mood to celebrate."

Mustela leaped from Tigress's shoulder to Dread's and bobbed her head up and down.

Dread stroked her neck. "See that? Mustela knows where the party is. Let's go get that drink girl. We about to be some Cave Maze heroes!"

Tigress and I stepped out into the brisk evening air.

"The Inn is just next door," I said. "You know William only lets registered questing team members stay here."

The Questers Inn was a small structure but stood out as the cleanest and most well kept in Trosworth. We showed the old man at the desk our keys and were waved up. Just as we got to the top of the stairs a random room door slammed shut.

Tigress inhaled a sharp breath and grabbed my hand tight. "I'm a little stressed out about tomorrow. I don't know how I'm going to get any sleep. I could really use a nightcap." She leaned close and whispered, "Do you still have some of that good honey mead?"

"I do, and a night cap with you will hit the spot for sure."

"I'll come to your room after I clean up," she said.

"I look forward to it Miss Tigress." Did Tigress want a nightcap to wind down before bed, or was this going to be a romantic interlude? She blew me off at her house, but this was neutral ground. Either way I liked where this was going.

My small room contained only a wooden framed bed and side table, which held a welcoming pitcher of water, two cups, and a brass washbowl. I flung my gear into the corner, washed up, and plopped down on the bed. A quiet knock brought me back to my feet. I opened the door to see a thing of beauty. Tigress smelled like moist fresh cut roses, and wore a skimpy chemise of thin, fine linen. My knees weakened. I now remember why I had such a crush on her while at the abbey.

"There is a God." I said.

Tigress pushed me aside and sat on the bed. "Boy you crazy."

I sat next to her and poured two shots of honey mead. "To a blessed run in the Cave Maze."

We clanked shots and took the drink immediately to the head. I poured another round. "There's plenty more where that came from."

Tigress leaned back into the bed. "Thank you Raff, I really needed that. Are you scared about tomorrow?"

"Not at all. That questing captain from the wagon is praying for us. We also have Chawett on the team now. We got as solid of a plan as there could be. I'm sure we will achieve our goal. After going through the five rooms my father listed, we'll have all the treasure we need. You and your mother should easily be able to purchase a new breading sniffer. Or two."

"You know Mustela likes you. She thinks we should be a couple. That means a lot because she doesn't like anybody that way for me."

I leaned on one elbow, sinking into the mattress and bedding. "I think Mustela is my favorite sniffer in the whole world right now. All I need is to get my dad to think that same way. He always made it clear to me that you are off limits. If you weren't obviously mixed with elf, I would think you might be my sister or something. I wonder if our parents ever messed around."

Tigress shook her head. "Knowing your dad they probably did."

"Messing around," I mumble. "There's a rumor amongst questers that a kiss from the girl of your dreams before a run makes for amazing luck, and sure riches."

Tigress clasped her hands in front of her and looked at her lap. "That's an interesting rumor. If the girl of your dreams were here, you could put it to the test."

I scooted in close and put my arm around her waist. "You know what? Right now you *are* the girl of my dreams."

BANG, BANG, BANG! The room rattled with a loud knock at the door. I jumped off the bed, grabbed my dagger and took a position near the handle. "Who's there?" I took a brief pause, then snapped the door open. I jumped into the hallway to find it empty. "Dread I know it's you! Stop playing!"

Tigress glided past me ducking into her room directly across the hall. She cracked open the door and peeked out, batting her eyes. "Goodnight Raff."

"Hey pretty girl, I was really looking forward to that good luck kiss."

Tigress tilted her head to the side and squinted. "Raff I know your daddy. They say like father, like son, and your father's a player. If I'm really the girl of your dreams then you'll get that kiss." She slowly licked her lips. "Besides, you said it yourself. We got a solid plan, so there's no luck needed to get these riches. Goodnight Raff."

"Damn Dread!" I yelled out loud. "You play too much!" I ran down the stairs to the inn's lobby. "Where are you?" I'd give that man a piece of my mind when I caught him.

The innkeeper was asleep. His chair propped against the wall, and his head cocked back over the top. I stepped outside and took a deep breath to calm down.

A man across the street pestered everyone that walked by. "Speak with a real live locked up hag! Only one gold coin!"

I latched onto the distraction or, rather, the reminder of my heritage. This could be a hoax, but I had to know more about hags. What if the magic inside of me could be deemed Cave Maze useful? I could be a magic user, and command their pay in the Maze. All the girls loved magic users too. I had to take a chance on this.

Across the street the man baited me in. "Right this way my friend. For one gold coin you can spend all the time you want questioning the hag. Some questers have got her to tell them of secret rooms in the Maze, while others have coxed her into divulging the recipe to make powerful potions."

"Is it safe?" I asked.

The man pulled a glassy stone with a natural hole in it from his pocket. "It is if you have this on your person. The adder stone will protect you from the witch. I have also placed a trough of crickets, mealworms, grubs, and waxworms in front of her cage. You must not cross it."

I pulled a coin from my pocket, and clinched it tight in my fist. "Is it a real hag?"

"You're a big, bad quester aren't you? If the hag is a fake you can come back here with your team and kill me. It's real, it's real, it is real." He inched closer to the building where the supposed hag resided.

"Here is your payment," I said. "Show me to the hag."

The man stuffed the coin is his pocket, and then strung the adder stone into a necklace. "Put this around your neck, and don't remove it. Also don't cross the trough." He patted me down. "Weapons?"

"I'm unarmed."

The man lifted five iron bars, and then pulled hard to open the heavy oak door. He then showed me down a stone stairwell lined with upside-down hanging brooms. At the bottom we took a sharp turn into a dungeon lit with only two torches. I couldn't see past the row of bars in front of me. "She talks to some, others nothing. Take your time with it." He walked up the stairs. "Knock on the door loudly when you are ready to be let out."

I sat on a wood stool and looked into the dark cage. "Hello."

Two flaky black and blue hands wrapped around the cage bars. The hag moaned and brought her face up between her hands. She had one dilated blood-red eye. The other was a swollen black slit dripping dark green slime down her face.

"Tell me a story of the Maze," she said in a cracked voice.

Her tart breath forced me to lean back. All that I had heard about a hag's breath was true, hers smelt like the foulest stench of forty thousand year funk. "I am one-fourth hag. And need to know how to harness it's magic."

"You are not a-fourth hag. You are a half succubus, a hag bastard. If you have any magic it will be foul and limited, but I sense you want it anyway. Remove that nasty stone, lie down next to the trough, and close your eyes. I will assess your abilities, if you have something we could arrange a trade."

I rolled the adder stone to the wall, laid down on the floor, and closed my eyes. The hag did the same in her cell, she moans, which soon turned into a wonderfully sung lullaby. I opened my eyes to see a beautiful smiling woman sitting cross-legged on the stool in the room with me. She wore only a white fur cloak.

"I am here to turn on your power to slip from your skin," she said softly. "Out of your skin you will be invisible, and able to float through cracks, crevices, and keyholes like a ghost. Eavesdropping on conversations can be a lucrative activity, slipping into a fair maiden's body while she sleeps can be exhilarating. Imagine making love to the most inaccessible princess in an exotic dream world."

I sit up. "Who are you? Where is the hag?"

The torches flickered and went dim. "The hag will activate your magic, but she will demand freedom from her cell first, something you can not provide. All I want is a piece of your affection as trade."

The woman was attractive, and I needed the power of magic. "Seems fair." I stood and faced the woman. She stood, dropped the cloak, and held both hands out my direction. "Yes, seems fair to me." I took her hands and pulled in close. When our bodies touched I blacked out.

CHAPTER 16

"Wake up!"

I opened my eyes to find the hag that was behind bars now standing above me. I strained to stand up but stumbled and fell against the wall. Short of breath, I ached all over, my back felt like it was on fire.

"That was fun." The hag's one eye bulged with popping red veins. "Your magic is now active, you can slip your skin once a year. Of course you must hag ride someone to death once a year also." All ten of the hag's fingernails grew into pointy black talons. "I'll be damned if I let you live to do either."

What did I do? How did she get free? I stumbled back toward the stairs. The moment I turned, her talons ripped across my calf, tearing my pants to shreds. "Help! Open the door!"

I continued to crawl up. The hag snatched my ankle and dragged me down. I kicked her hard in the face, she spun and smacked into a bundle of broom straw. She tore the broom off the wall, and then sat down cross-legged counting each strand, one by one.

Bars lifted above, the man opened the door. "What's all this racket?" He looked down the stairwell at me shaking his head. "I told you not to cross the trough!"

I looked at him, then down the stairs at the hag. *Was I just calling for help?* This would make me look bad, I got to do something. "That's right hag! Count straw." I limped up the stairs as quick as I could, leaving drops of blood dripping from my calf.

The man draped a necklace with several adder stones around his neck, and then took a few steps down toward the hag. "You're lucky to have made it on the stairwell. This old hag can't resist counting the straws of a broom."

I looked down at the scene from the top of the stairs and clenched my calf. "Yeah, lucky is right."

The man pointed at me. "Hey, hey you took off the adder stone. I specifically told you not to do that. It's going to take me a long time to get this thing back in her cage. You owe me another gold coin for the trouble."

I made a hard right turn out of the door, limped far down the road and sat on a bench. What just happened? Was I a magic user now? I didn't feel like a magic user. That man must have just hustled me. The whole thing had to have been staged.

A short figure draped in a black cloak knelt down in front of me. "Baby you okay?"

"Who is you?" I asked.

"It's me, Porridge." She lifted her hood. "You leg looks bad, what have you been into?"

Porridge. So it wasn't a dream. "Well I—"

She held a finger to my lips. "Shh, don't even worry about it." She wrapped a cloth gently around my wound and tied it. "You're pale, it looks like you can really use a drink. I know a place, let's go."

Arm in arm, we walked down a dark back alley to an unassuming wooden door with no handle. Porridge knocked three times and it opened. "This is Ye Old Trip to Salutation, a pub where the more ambitious habitants of the Light Woods gather."

This medium-sized square room had five wood-cross chandeliers hanging from the ceiling, each with several large candles lit on top. Three very different bars were on each side of the room.

The one on the right was of a tiny scale, and tended by a female pixie about the size of my hand. She wore a sparkling green outfit with a matching pointed hat topped with a bell. She danced down the bar while wiping it down with a rag. The bar in front of us was waist-high, and sat in front of the soft sandstone rock that the building is set against. A stubby gnome with a white beard and red conical hat served the two gnomes that sat there. The bar to the left was of standard proportion, and tended by a pretty blond human girl.

A short rusting iron gate mounted into sandstone wall creaked open. A gnome appeared from the cave behind it carrying a small wooden model ship. He placed it on the bar. "I give you this as payment for my tab. Hang this galleon up high above the bar. It will bring good luck to your establishment as long as you don't clean it."

The blond girl waved our direction. "Over here, beautiful!"

Porridge pulled me that direction. "That's my friend. Come on Raff."

"Wait, wait." I tugged against her pull, but my heart wasn't in it. I felt so…drained. "How did you get here, Porridge?"

"I have my ways." She steered me toward a stool and I took a seat at the blonde's bar. Porridge stood next to me and smiled. "Two honey meads Annabella. My man here turned me on to the drink."

"Excellent choice," she said. "Your man knows his stuff."

Porridge removed her cloak and hung it on a nearby coat stand. She wore shapely brown leather armor, a strap with several small bottles, and a sheathed dagger hanging from it. "Now let me take a closer look at that wound." She gently rewrapped my calf. "It's really just a scratch, you're going to be fine."

I set a hand on her shoulder, thankful for her care, but still confused. "What brings you into Trosworth? I didn't think brownies were that adventurous."

"Raff, have you noticed that I'm not like other brownies?"

"Oh I've noticed all right. You are the finest brownie I have ever seen, and taller too."

"That's because I'm part tree sprite, what you know as a dryad."

"Wow. Part brownie, part dryad. I really like that combination. That's beautiful."

"That combination really likes you too," she said. "I'm sorry if I interrupted you and Tigress at the Inn earlier, but when I saw her enter your room with sexy attire I was worried. I wouldn't want you to end up tongue kissing your sister…or worse, that would be just nasty."

"Tigress isn't my sister."

"The woman you know as Tigress' mother really is not. Tigress is the product of your father and an elf girl."

First hags and now this? "How would you know that?"

"As a brownie-dryad I socialize with all the inhabitants of the Light Woods, including the always talkative elves." She glanced up at me, blinking slow the way she did when she first came to my room. "Are you surprised about Tigress?"

"Actually no, my father does get around." Once again my dad's past dealt me a blow. Tigress had always been a great friend, and this ensured it would stay that way, friends. Now I could concentrate on this sexy vision right here-a brownie-dryad, mixed just like me. "You know I recently found out I'm mixed too, with hag."

"You're not mixed with hag Raff, you're mixed with succubus. I am part brownie so I can sense what you are. And what you are is good at heart, not at all hag."

"Hag, succubus. It's all bad isn't it?"

"Annabella here is a succubus. She has been my friend for a long time, and she's all-good. I know hag, they *are* a problem."

Annabella smiled at me. I couldn't help but smile back. She didn't seem too bad, especially if she really *was* a succubus.

"My problem with hags is they're buying all the huo-yao out from under me. What problem do you have with them?"

Porridge returned to bandaging my wound. "There's constant fighting between the habitants of the Light Woods and the hags. Those barbaric bitches capture pixies, and then give them to Talhoffer, who compresses the poor things into a liquid."

"Yuck, what does he do, drink it?"

"When the liquid is mixed with huo-yao it creates a toxic smoke he exposes to fleas. His plan is to infect black rats with the fleas, and release them into the Kingdom of Evonland. The rats will go mad with the toxin and bite the Evons, infecting them. The result will be a sweeping death across there territory."

"Well I for one hope Talhoffer whips those biting disease-rats on them quick! It would be nice to avoid war with the Evons. If they're all wiped out, we're all good."

"You don't understand what the disease does, and how contagious it is. The pestilence will spread into Broxington and wipe us all out. Talhoffer will be the only one with the cure, and he will only make it available to his hag, orc, and freakish cohorts. The man wants the whole island to himself, from Evonland to Broxington."

Talhoffer was out to eradicate everyone on the island? There went my future as a quester. "I guess if Talhoffer succeeds he will finally have that seclusion he desires."

"If Talhoffer succeeds we will all be dead." She tied the ends of my bandage into a knot. "Which brings me to the favor I was trying to ask of you at Tigress' house. I am part of an alliance that is dedicated to protecting the small community of pixies that still exists. I need you to join us in helping to save them. Saving the pixies will also stop Talhoffer from producing the toxin, for now."

This sounded like a tall order. How did a run for tuition gold turn into this?

Porridge took my hand. "There is a bonus to my favor Raff. Members of the alliance gain access to an underground tavern called The Victoria Inn. It's so exciting there. They have melodious music, savory cuisine, complex wines, and some really exotic accommodations. It would be a nice place for a first date."

"I do like exotic accommodations, we have got to make that happen." A date with Porridge in a place like this could be the start of something special. She was way more my type then that whorish Vixenett back home. Prettier too.

"We *can* make that happen Raff, but you need to be a member of the alliance to gain entrance. Are you okay with joining us?"

"I am more than willing to do *anything* for the fine young lady who just saved my leg."

"Thank you Raff!" She wrapped her arms around my neck. "I feel you can make a difference. It's also how I know there is not a drop of hag in you."

"So what exactly is it I can do to help?"

She looked at Annabella and smiled. "My succubus connection passed word that Talhoffer has several pixies caged in a room in the Maze. This room is said to be somewhere in the vicinity of a long rumored service entrance. If you find this room, it would mean a lot if you could set them free."

"We have a very specific plan for our run in the Maze. I will keep an eye out, but I can't promise we will find this room."

Annabella put both elbows on the bar, clasp her hands, and rested her chin on top. "I got more information for you. Where you find the pixies, you will find Talhoffer's amassment of huo-yao."

"This task just got better," I say. "I need huo-yao."

"Free the pixies and collect the huo-yao," Porridge said. "You will be on your way to legendary questing captain status."

"Why don't you join my team Porridge? We will have to upgrade your armor. Yours leaves some areas unprotected."

She lifted her corset. "I'm a child of the trees Raff, and would not be much good to you underground. My roll with the alliance is like a spy."

"A spy makes sense, being part dryad you can probably hide in a tree if you need to."

"I love the trees, but I can't step into them like full blood dryads do. My father says I have more brownie traits than dryad. He taught me how to blend into just about anything quickly though. Since I am half brownie, I am invisible to several demonic beings, like the undead and cockatrice. Hags can't even see me, although they can smell my presence. What I can do is teleport to various trees around Broxington. That's how I got here. All I have to do is drink from one of these."

She unhooked a bottle from her strap. "Each one takes me to a different tree, in a different place. I currently have connections from Rettingham to Tickhill. I hope to soon form a bond with an old cypress in Woodthorpe, it would be my first oversea connection."

"That's a great way to get around. Where does the one in your hand take you?"

"A sip from this bottle will have me step out of a young sapling near the Entry Cave to the Maze."

The Maze. I dropped a gold coin down on the bar. "I need to sleep off this drink, and this injury. Annabella you're amazing."

I got off my stool, stumbled and grabbed my calf. "Ahh!" Porridge came in quick and close to stop me from falling. I took her in my arms and looked into her eyes. "And once again you save me."

She looked up at me low through her long lashes. "I did kind of save you again."

"Annabella, I need a bottle of that mead to go. Porridge, this injury is starting to hinder my ability to walk. I can really use your help to get up to my room."

Porridge locked arms with me and took the bottle from Annabella. "I got you baby."

As I opened the pub door the bar pixie zipped to Porridge's shoulder and spoke into her ear. "Uh-oh, I got to go Raff. The alliance needs me."

There went my plan for midnight company. "I need you too. My leg, remember?"

Porridge twirled a glistening strand of hair around her finger. "Rumor has it that a kiss from the girl of your dreams before a run makes for amazing luck and sure riches."

I pulled Porridge's frame in close. "Well I could use some amazing luck and sure riches. And I think I got a dream girl in front of me right now. Porridge, can you bless me with that kiss?"

I brought her in close and sunk into the softest lips.

Annabella tickled Porridge's side breaking up our embrace. "Get a room you two."

Porridge laughed and nudged her away. "I will see you again soon Raff. Look to the trees."

I walked back to the inn turning the mead bottle up as I went. Once in my room I flung myself onto the bed. Okay, time to think… *Porridge, pixies, huo-yau, and the Cave Maze in the morning.* How was I going to tell Tigress that we were related? I sucked the bottle dry and passed out cold.

※ ※ ※

An annoying chorus of rooster crowing woke me. I groggily dragged myself to the window and spread the curtains. The early morning sun blasted me as I looked out over the high road. Questers loaded up horses and wagons for their respective runs. I went to retrieve my clothes from the corner and found them cleaned and crisply folded. A plate of hot honey mint crisples sits by my bed. *Thanks William. They really take care of you at this Inn.*

Down in the tavern I found Tigress at the bar staring into a steaming bowl. To my eyes, she was still sexy but…in a sisterly sort of way now. I tapped her on the shoulder. "Good morning, how's the gruel?"

Her nose wrinkled. "Horrible stuff, It can use a heap of honey, but they have none. How did you sleep last night?"

"Unsatisfying at best thank you. Where's Mustela? I hope Dread didn't keep her out all night."

Tigress pushed away the nearly full bowl. "They're both in the gamblers area."

A man approached from behind the bar. "Gruel for you sir?"

I looked down into Tigress bowl of lumpy gray slop. "Oh hell no. Let's go check that tote board Tigress. I can't wait to see our team listed on it."

Only a few gamblers milled on the floor this early, they studied the boards and took notes. Dread stared up at the center tote board with a stack of gold coins tightly pinched between his finger and thumb.

"Good morning, cousin. And may I ask how you came upon that lovely stack of early morning gold coins?"

Dread did not turn his head from looking up at the tote board. "I hustled some of Castillo's team members at the shell game last night."

"Well done," I said. "If you're looking to parlay that gold I got a hot tip on a team from Beeston for you. I see our over-under number has been set at four."

"I can absolutely understand the four," Dread said. "But William put the *total slaughter* bet in effect on our team."

"What's a total slaughter bet?" Tigress asked. "That sounds bad."

Dread's head dropped down. "That means the odds maker thinks there's a good chance our whole team will get killed on this run. It's rare the house offers up this bet, it's typically reserved for extreme lowlife questing teams."

"I'll take that bet all day Dread," I said. "Remember, William doesn't know how good our map is, or how fool-proof of a strategy we got. Here he comes now, with Chaz, and Chawett."

"Looks to me like team Beeston is ready." William said. "I took a lot of action on your team last night. I expect to see you all back here in one piece after your run."

Dread pushed past William. "Yes Sir. Lets get on the road and make that happen." He walked out of the tavern door.

William put his arm around my shoulder. "Dread seams a bit on edge. A lot of questers get like that before their first run.

Putnum rushed to Williams's side, handed him a betting slip, and took off the other direction. William looked the slip over, "Yes, yes! Before leaving you should go over my newly revised prop bets." He lowered his voice. "I have word team Rettingham is getting close to finding a Talhoffer item. Seventy-five to one would make some nice pocket gold for you Raff."

"Yea, it would." I peek at William's slip and catch a glimpse of another bet-'Odds a captain will be killed'- I am the three-to-one favorite. The team didn't need to see this.

I pushed the slip away and headed for the door. "No time for all that. Come on team, let's catch up with Dread."

LAIS DIJON TAVERN:
ODDS ON TEAMS ENTERING THE CAVE MAZE.

Team: Gabbiano - Death Over/Under: 6
From: Rettingham
Members: 21
Map Level: 10/10
(Said to contain secret shortcuts deep into the Maze.)
Key personnel: Captain Castello Gabbiano (Fighter)
Slyslick Wicked (Enchanter)
Bonnaroo Grifter (Thief)
Monjo Grifter (Belette)
Gnarly Nouman (Thief)
Fergus Slymar (Fighter)
*Last run in Team Gabbiano lost 5/23, the previous 4/20.
*No team lead by Captain Gabbiano has ever lost more then 6 members.
*Slyslick can cast his spike bombardment spell often.

Team: Rettingham - Death Over/Under: 6
From: Rettingham
Members: 20
Map Level: 8/10
(Has been passed down through many generations of the Sandby family)
Key personnel: Captain Percy Sandby (Fighter)
Clive Bywater (Sorcerer)
Dudley Southall (Fighter)
Tica Fitzturgis (Belette)
Horace Codswallop (Thief)
Thor Goodslog (Fighter)
*Last run in Team Rettingham lost 4/20, the previous 2/20.
*This run's team features an outstanding core of five magic users.
*Percy Sandby's conservative tendencies could save lives during a time when the Maze is hot.

Team: Greensludge - Death Over/Under: 3
From: Parts Unknown
Members: 7
Map Level: 6/10
(This patchwork map could yield unexpected gain.)
Key personnel: Captain Pleiades Greensludge (Fighter)
Mofo Fomo (Soothsayer)
Crhymes Boozer (Thief)
Hans Barleycorn (Fighter)
Tawaif Yoshiwara (Belette)
Chugalug Pissup (Thief)
*This is a newly formed team of unconventional veterans.
*Mofo Fomo's excellent defensive spells should keep them out of trouble.
*Captain Greensludge vows to take this team deeper then any six-man team has ventured before.

Team: Beeston - Death Over/Under: 4
Special wager in effect: Total slaughter odds 9-1
From: Beeston
Members: 6
Map Level: 0/10 (House Map)
Key personnel: Captain Raff Orcslaughter (Fighter)
Chawett Loinchop (Soothsayer)
Chazekiel Manor (Fighter)
Tigress Moet (Fighter)
Mustela Moet (Belette)
Dread Jenkins (Thief)
*Five of this teams six members are amateurs, a total slaughter is tenable.
*Teams only experienced member is a bottom of the board magic user.
*Mustela Moet has given birth to several top sniffers, but has never been in the Maze herself.

Team: O'Grady - Death Over/Under: 6
From: St. Brigitte (Woodthorpe)
Members: 21
Map Level: 9/10
(Said to contain routing to constantly replenished gold depositories.)
Key personnel: Captain Finnegas O'Grady (Fighter)
Swoggle Whaley (Thief)
Lucky Kavanach (Belette)
Buck Shiels (Fighter)
Leanan Morrigan (Enchanter)
Hooley Stout (Fighter)
*Last run in Team O'Grady lost 4/20, the previous 4/20.
*Captain O'Grady may have to venture uncomfortably deeper in the Maze for gold this run.
*Leanan's poisonous chants can mean a quick death to male foes.

Team: Questiarum University - Death Over/Under: 8
From: Tickhill
Members: 23
Map Level: 7/10
(Said to contain quick and easy access to the gold rich southwest region of the Maze.)
Key personnel: Captain Tatlen Hall (Fighter)
Skirrid de Bussel (Enchanter)
Sivarat Swardswinger (Fighter)
Jibber Budworth (Belette)
Edward Eerie III (Thief)
Cecilia Cynan (Fighter)
*Last run in the Questiarum University team lost 7/21, the previous 6/22.
*This team is a mixed bag of both crafty veterans, and first time amateurs.
*The area of the Maze Captain Hall is known to frequent has been especially deadly as of late.

Odds subject to change.

LAIS DIJON TAVERN:
FUTURES AND PROPS:

ODDS A TALHOFFER ITEM WILL BE FOUND:
Beeston / 350 to 1 (Don't belong in the conversation.)
Greensludge / 200 to 1
Questiarum University / 200 to 1
O'Grady / 150 to 1 (More into gold then items.)
Rettingham / 75 to 1
Gabbiano / 25 to 1 (Best map in the game.)

ODDS A SNIFFER WILL BE KILLED:
Lucky Kavanach (O'Grady) / 200 to 1
(Team O'Grady has never lost a sniffer.)
Tica Fitzturgis (Rettingham) / 175 to 1
Monjo Grifter (Gabbiano) / 150 to 1
Jibber Budworth (Questiarum U.) / 50 to 1
(Heavy death toll over last few runs.)
Tawaif Yoshiwara (Greensludge) / 35 to 1
Mustela Moet (Beeston) / 15 to 1
(Should leave questing to the offspring.)

ODDS A CAPTAIN WILL BE KILLED:
Gabbiano / 350 to 1
Sandby (Rettingham) / 175 to 1
(Five magic users of protection.)
O'Grady / 175 to 1
Hall (Questiarum University) / 85 to 1
Greensludge / 45 to 1
(Recklessness often equals deadness.)
Orcslaughter (Beeston) / 3 to 1
(Dead man/team running.)

Odds subject to change.

CHAPTER 17

Trosworth was far behind us when we came to a three-way fork in the road. Option one: the Elvin Toll Road. It wound gently into the sunny Light Woods. Option two: the Trollebotten Path. It zigzagged into the dark Thorneywood Forest.

We walked away from both. *Our* course took us on the third and much less traveled option: the Carling Trail.

Everyone gathered around me as I unrolled the map. "Up the Carling Trail, through the Thorneywood Forest, then along the Trollebotten River to the ruins."

Chawett looked over the map. "This is good. The Carling trail goes around the back of the troll's main territory. Our best chance at avoiding any encounters will be to make the ruins well before nightfall."

Chaz pushed his way through us to the start of the trail. He spread apart some brush with his hands. "Gold is calling and you all are still back there? Come on."

The dense forest thinned and the sunrays beat through the branches. Our dark trail soon came to an opening where the water interrupted the forest silence.

"Oh yah!" Dread ran to the river and sat on a smooth rock along its bank. After prying off his boots he stuck both feet in the water. "Ahhhh, there we go. Half way to the ruins and it's time to let the bunions breathe."

Chaz, Chawett, and I joined him on the rocks. I splashed some refreshing cold water on my face and filled my flask. Tigress followed a prancing Mustela up along the banks where the forest met the river.

"Where they going?" Dread asked.

"I would say Mustela smells something," Chawett said. "Look at the trees, there's something coming through the—"

Smash! A young boy burst through the forest ahead of Tigress. His tangled brown hair streamed behind him in his haste. As he flashed by, I caught a glimpse of his pointed ears. One had a large ring pierced into the tip. A wood elf. He ran at top speed alongside the river. His little legs pumped in a blur and he looked desperately out of breath.

Crashing behind him busted out a towering greenish-brown troll. It high-stepped on the elf's heals. Mustela jumped on Tigress's shoulder. Before any of us could gather our wits or belongings, Tigress sprinted after the troll.

Chaz stood and stomped a foot into the ground. "That is not our business Tigress! Stop following them!"

This was the first troll I'd seen and the stories barely did it justice. Dread jammed on his boots and leapt up. "Lets go team. That little elf is going to need some help."

"I'm with you," Chawett said.

The elf cut swiftly back into the forest. The troll continued directly behind him without missing a step. The monster swept his lanky arms wildly from left to right, cutting down all forestry in its path.

When the three of us caught up we found Tigress deep in the forest dug in behind some thick brush. Her bow was drawn tight and pointed through some branches. We took up position next to her and peered through the shrubbery. The elf was on his back lodged under the troll's foot. I could barely see his head sticking up between two of the beast's ghastly sharp talons.

Tigress viewed the scene with an unrelenting stare. "The troll caught the elf and dragged him to this clearing. I'm going to put this arrow through its neck. Be ready, when I have a clear shot it's on."

Chaz strolled up, crunching leaves and twigs underfoot, barely lessening his pace. "What is wrong with you fools? This is not our fight. You're wasting time on this stupid elf." He pulled my shoulder back. "There's nothing to gain here Raff."

I shook off Chaz's hand. "Consider this a warm-up for the Maze. Now get your weapon ready."

Chawett nodded, "Let's do it then." He rubbed his hands together in a circular motion creating a small red-hot ball the size of a hummingbird egg. "As soon as Tigress lets the arrow go we attack."

Chaz crossed his arms over his chest. "I will guard the rear." Could he sound any more bored?

The young elf seemed to detect Chawett's magic. He turned his head our direction as he squirmed and fought to get away.

The troll cocked its head back and let out a booming "Hawwwwch!" It then began to twitch in an effort to regurgitate the deadly stomach acid that would soon be vomited onto the elf's cranium.

"No," Tigress snarled.

She let her arrow launch at maximum velocity. It whizzed toward the troll's neck but curved up to buzz its head and lodge into the tree behind it. Fortunately for the elf, Dread and I were already in quick pursuit. I slashed my sword across the troll's leg, a putrid pea green juice sprayed as the troll wailed. The elf scampered away from the fight gasping for breath.

The now one-legged Troll stumbled backward but dealt a heavy backhand to Dread, who was just able to block it with his shield. Chawett rolled his Lava Sphere at our combatant hitting its torso with a burst of flame. The troll let out a booming yowl that was stifled when Tigress scissored her trident daggers across the hobbled beast's neck, beheading it. The troll smashed back against the trees, hacked up and sizzling from the fire.

"Yah that!" I said. "We made quick work of this nasty heifer."

Chawett patted me on the back. "Consider us all warmed up for the Maze."

Dread moaned. "Don't worry. I'm sure I'll be fine over here."

Chawett and I ran over to the thicket of bushes Dread had been launched into.

"Are you all right?" I asked.

Dread picked himself up and kneeled in front of a small wooden lockbox. He spat dirt, and pulled twisted branches from his hair. "I'm more than all right. I landed on a treasure chest. That stupid son of a bitch backhanded me right into it."

Mustela sniffed around the box while Tigress went to console the elf.

I tried to fight back my smile. "You know what Dread? That troll slapped the snot out of you player."

"Quiet Raff." Dread said. "I need to concentrate on this lock." Mustela chirped three times, then jumped on Dread's shoulder. "Thank you girl, I got the perfect tool for that." He pulled a long curved slide key from his pouch. "The poison needles in this chest will hail in all directions if I don't do this right. First lift, then rotate."

Chaz prodded the burnt up troll's belt with his sword. A large knobbed club and small pouch hung from it. "Anything in that pouch Chaz?" I called out. He pulled something out of it but kept it in the palm of his hand. "What's that—"

"I got it open, Raff!" Dread said. "And there's gold in here! Gold!"

I turned to the chest and examined its contents. There were a few dirty gold coins, a couple of empty triangle shaped glass bottles, and a thin wooden stick with a curve at one end.

Dread picked up the stick and looked it over with a scowl. "So eight measly gold coins and this dumb thing."

Chawett's mouth dropped wide open. "Mind your thoughts while that's in your hand Dread. I can't believe our good fortune. Do you know what you have there? It's a *wish* stick!"

"A wish stick." Dread cocked an eyebrow. "What's a wish stick?"

"Listen close." Chawett's voice quivered. "What you need to do is think real hard about an item you've wished for all your life. Quick though, did you think of it yet?"

Dread gripped the stick hard. "Yes. I thought of something. Now what?"

Chawett stood in front of Dread with his hands out to block any possible distractions. "Okay Dread, are you sure you're ready? Have you thought of something really good?"

Dread stood up straight. "Yes, yes I have. I'm ready. What next?"

"Here we go then," Chawett said. "What I need you to do, is 'stick' that worthless thing in the air and 'wish' it had had some magic power. 'Wish-stick', Ha Ha! I got you Dread!"

Dread froze in place with the stick held up high.

Chawett snatched the stick from Dread's deceived hand. "I know exactly what this is used for." He closed his eyes, tilted his head up, and scratched his butt with the curved end of the stick. "This is one fancy backscratcher."

"You wrong for that Chawett," I said. Treasure chests didn't hold worthless junk. That stick did *something*. We just needed to figure out what.

Dread grabbed the stick from Chawett and tucked it into his belt. "You got jokes huh? Just the other day my back itched in a place I couldn't reach, I could have used a stick like this."

Chawett opened up a small purple velvet bag with gold drawstrings. "Here you go Dread, put the gold in here."

Dread dropped the coins in the bag. Chawett pulled the drawstrings then tossed the bag in the air.

Dread caught it and held it up. "Nice coin purse."

"That's not a coin purse," Chawett said. "It's a heavynessless bag, and is capable of holding over five thousand coins without a gain in weight or mass. All of us Cave Maze veterans have one of these to keep our riches."

"No, no, no!" Chaz pointed his finger in Chawett's face. "You are a Cave Maze jester, and an idiot for nominating a thief to hold my-I mean *our*-gold. I am the one financing this run, so I will be the one holding the bounty. Now give it up thief." Chaz reached for the bag.

Dread yanked it away. "You about to pull back a nub trying to snatch a thief's booty sack."

"Calm down gentlemen," Chawett said. "Cave Maze protocol is that a team's thief always carries the bounty. With the amount of pickpockets in and around the Maze you would get peeled back of that bag like a banana Chaz. You're a fighter so you need to concentrate on fighting. A good thief like Dread will never get his pocket picked."

Dread tied the bag to his belt. "That's right Chaz. Know your Cave Maze protocol son." He grabbed his crotch. "You can hold this *nut* sack though."

Mustela spun and sprung up onto Tigress' shoulder. She pointed her nose up and made a frantic screech. An owl the size of a horse swooped down to the clearing with a blast of wind. It let out a high-pitched shriek and rotated its head around the area.

I drew my sword and took cover near a tree. It looked at me with dark orange eyes and clucked rapidly.

"Lower your weapons!" Tigress said. "It's okay! The owl is with the elf."

Tigress lifted the young elf onto the owl. He pulled a strap from under its yellowish-brown plumage and dug in his heels. The owl shrieked and flew up in a tunnel of wind.

Chaz ran after the owl and threw a rock at it. "If it was up to me you would have a mouth full of steamy troll vomit elf!" He looked at Tigress and shook his fist. "That's gratitude for you. Not even a thank you from that unappreciative little misfit."

He stomped over to me and stood in my face. "We just risked our lives, threw off our schedule, and used up a percentage of Chawett's precious magic power for what? A few measly gold coins and a butt-scratching stick? That's just pitiful! Now let's get back to the run."

Chawett kicked the troll's severed head. "We do need to get out of here. This troll will regenerate before long, and he's sure to be upset.

It would be good if we are far, far away from this area when that happens."

We retraced our steps back toward the river. Once out of the forest the sun was close to setting. Chawett and Chaz took the lead moving along the river at a pace twice the speed as before. Tigress and I kept a slight distance behind them with Dread lagging in the rear.

"Remember,"-Chawett looked back at us, and then into the trees with a concerned eye-"we got to make the ruins before nightfall."

"So Tigress," I asked. "What was that little elf talking to you about? Why was he so deep in the forest?"

Tigress stroked Mustela who slept comfortably around her neck. "The poor thing was so shaken, I could barely understand him. I did get that his name was Tomte, and that he was with a band of young elves from the Light Woods. They were trying to complete some sort of overnight elf test to become warriors. Trolls ambushed their camp and they all scattered. Apparently Tomte was being chased for quite some distance when he popped out at the river."

"Well he sure was lucky," I said. "Lucky he ran into us."

It was well after sunset when we set up camp at the Carling Ruins. The foundations of only a few buildings and a long fallen column were all that remained.

Tigress and I gathered wood and dry grass to make fire. I heard some prowling in the trees, and spotted what looked like yellow eyes blinking in the distant bush. "The undead would feel right at home in this place."

Chaz struck a chunk of flint to a piece of wood embedded with steel. He struck it several times only producing a few faint sparks. "Damn little elf."

"No need to work that flint so hard Chaz," Chawett said. "You got a magic user here, I've been flicking finger fire since I was two." Chawett prepared to flick his thumb.

Chaz backed him off. "No Chawett! You have already wasted enough of your magic power on that pissy ass elf incident. I'll light the fire my way, you need to save everything you got to deal with the killers in that Maze. I mean look at you, what good are you with no magic?"

Chawett unstrapped a shinny black stick from his belt and held it forward.

"Uh-huh," Chaz adjusted the piece of wood. "You have a walking stick for defense."

"A shillelagh," Chawett pounded the knobbed end in his hand. "This end is loaded with molten lead. I can administer quite a beating with this if I must."

Chaz struck the flint again and the fire came to life. *Finally*, I thought. We all passed out by the long overdue flames.

As I slept a quite voice whispered in my ear. "Don't open your eyes, no matter what you do."

The Cockatrice

CHAPTER 18

I tried to lift my arms but I was too weak. Short of breath, my chest felt like it was on fire. I knew that voice.

"There's a cockatrice perched on your chest," said the voice. "It's staring you down, so don't open your eyes. You'll be turned to stone immediately if you do." A soft, wet tongue licked in my ear.

"Is that you Porridge?" I kept my eyes squeezed tight.

"Yes it is baby, I've been with you all this time. Nice moves on that troll back in the forest."

"I can't move."

"Shhhh, the cockatrice has paralyzed you with its poison breath. It also has a spur lined up at your neck, so stay calm. Mustela has been alerted, and will thrash this vulture for trying to mess with *my* man."

Skrawwww! A pounding collision lifted the pressure from my chest. I opened my eyes but still could not move a muscle.

Mustela locked up with the goose-sized cockatrice and rolled across the ground. Her eyes flared fiery red as she hissed, barked, and clawed the cock at every opening. Our belette's lightning-fast quickness blocked the cock's claw and bite attack, but was unable to deal with its scaly snake tail. Several whips slashed her body and face including a blood-splattering one across her nose.

Dread and Tigress rushed toward the scene.

"Stay back!" Chawett said. "Mustela's immune to the cock's

deadliest offenses, we are not. A drop of that thing's blood will burn through your sword, shield, flesh, and bone."

Mustela clamped a bite down on the evil bird's neck, then ripped and tugged violently. They slid down a bank and slammed into a tree, directly on Mustela's head. The cock righted itself and then sprinted forward, flapping its wings for take off. With Mustela still dangling on its neck, the powerful cock clumsily elevated them both to the crest of the forest trees. The fight was ended there when Mustela wrapped her body around the bird's head and twisted. A loud crack echoed down when the cock's neck snapped. The two animals spun out together down through the branches and crashed into a deep clump of bush.

Mustela's head popped up from under the pile. She made two giant hops away from the mess into Tigress' arms. Tigress held her tight and gave a gentle rub behind the ears.

I made another attempt to get up but a wave of hot nausea knocked me back to the ground. Where did Porridge go? Was she okay? That sexy girl just saved my life. Definitely a keeper.

Chawett looked down at me and smiled. "You know what? That just may be a Rex Goliath over there."

Dread took my hand and lifted me up. My stomach bubbled and head felt hot.

Chawett looked into my eyes. "The whole poison feeling won't last long, you will be all right shortly. Does anyone have a mirror? I want to check this dirty bird out."

Chaz wiped the sleep out of his eyes. "I have one, but I am not going near that thing." He handed Chawett a small ornate mirror. "Don't break it."

I put my arm around Dread's neck for stability. We then followed our magic user into the bush. There was no way I was going to miss getting a look at this creature.

Chawett approached the dead beast using the mirror to guide him in. "This is an exceptionally big cockatrice. I really think it could be a Rex. Dread, hold the mirror in the exact position I give it to you. My son of a butcher upbringing will be good for something today."

Chawett unsheathed a small dagger and sliced off the bird's head. He then mashed and rubbed it against a nearby tree. "Blood is drained." He took the mirror from Dread's hand and held the severed head to it. "Look in the mirror, its eyes are still alive with the power to stone. Something like this could be useful in the Maze."

"How long is its stoning power going to last?" I asked.

Chawett looked deep into the cock's twitching black eyeball reflection. "With a bird this big, I would guess at least three or four days. Open up the heavynessless bag Dread, we're going to need a safe place to keep this." Chawett held one hand over the head's probing eyes and dropped it into the bag.

A muffled cracking and popping came from the dead cock's body. Dread and I stepped back. "What's happening, what's that noise?"

Chawett dropped to his knees and began plucking quills. "The body's turning to stone!" He managed to pull a dozen quills off before the headless bird was a complete white stone statue. He sat on the ground out of breath. "We could have something here, Dread, open the bag."

Chawett stuffed all but two of the feathers into the heavynessless bag. The two he didn't put in were the largest of the bunch, and the only ones with a purple tinge. He pulled the ostrich feathers out of his hat, and tucked the cockatrice feathers in.

"That's a slick look for you Chawett," I said.

"I know this," he said. "But it's more than just a good look. If this was a Rex Goliath then these quills could be worth a lot of gold to the right wizard. You see there are certain deviant spells that only can be written using the quills of a Goliath family cockatrice. Only one spell can be written per quill, they're very rare. Moe can authenticate these at the store back in Trosworth."

I almost told him to take the two out of his hat and put them in the bag, but he had the most knowledge of all of us. Without him, we wouldn't even have thought to take the feathers. Since no one else brought it up, I left the matter alone.

As we walked back to camp a sharp pain lurched in my stomach. I doubled over and blew chunks to the forest floor.

Dread patted me on the back. "It's a good thing Mustela was on the job back there, you were about to wake up stone cold Raff."

"I think I have bruised ribs," I said. "I also feel woozy from that thing's reeking poison breath." I put my hand on Dread's shoulder and lowered my voice. "Did you see a real cute brownie girl around here?" I should've been asking Tigress since the brownie family came from her house, but after what Porridge told me about Tigress and I being brother and sister, I'd rather not have to explain.

"A what?" Dread asked. "No cousin, I didn't. That cockatrice really messed your head up didn't it? Got you seeing things."

"I'm going to need a long sit down to regain my senses."

"Yes you are Raff," Dread said. "Tigress, how's my cousin's little savior doing?"

She pinched and fed Mustela a bluish-green herb. "This rue will help her recover from the poison, but there's a small scratch across her nose I'm worried about. I have a bad feeling it's going to cause her some trouble sniffing."

Chaz ran over to Tigress and exhaled loudly. He got in Mustela's face. "Damn it, that's just great. Look at the size of that gaping gash." He stood tall, stiff, and with a blank stare. "We got a sniffer that can not sniff."

Tigress gently pulled Mustela away. "She will be just fine with a little time Chaz. You already know she is a quick healer."

My stomach lurched and I spat puke up once again. I dropped down on my knees and attempted to heave out the toxin.

"This is really bad," Chaz scoffed. "I hope you cripples don't need this much time to recover *every* time you get into a little scuffle. We got real monsters to fight ahead of us, and you two are ailing from some chicken fight. I'm ready to cross this river and see if that map of yours is the truth or not."

I took a seat along the Trollebotten riverbank. Two tall broken columns rose from the middle, the last standing evidence of what was once a crude bridge washed out long ago.

Dread sat next to me, took off his boots, and massaged his feet in the chilly healing water. "This raw patch on my big toe is a major problem."

Tigress stood next to Dread, glanced down at his feet, then turned away gagging.

I unrolled the map and looked up into the hills. "The notes here say to look between these two pillars and line up a large boulder on the third plateau. The service entrance should be in the hillside there.

"I see the plateau," Tigress said. "I hope we can find some semblance of a path to help us cut through that bush."

Dread frowned and splashed his feet. "That's a steep climb."

Chaz looked up at the plateau, then down at Dread's feet. "Your hairy, gnarled, swollen feet disgust me Dread. What are you, part hobbit?"

"Your momma's part hobbit ya prissy son-of-a-bitch," Dread snapped.

"Come on now." My stomach finally seemed settled. "With all the gold we're going to lug back, Dread will have a cushioned pair of boots for those battered things in no time."

We easily cross the river and make our way up a semi beaten path. Once on the plateau we all examined the hill for the Cave Maze opening.

"This is it!" Dread ran to a section of vines hanging along the stone face. "There're some fresh tracks here too, this entrance hasn't been totally abandon."

Chaz kicked up some dirt around the tracks. "Secret entrance, and fresh tracks do not mix. Anyone could be in there."

Did my dad share the map with someone else? All of the gold in the rooms he indicated were probably pillaged a long time ago if he did. These tracks could be from the hags that brought pixies and huo-yao to Talhoffer. Are we a strong enough team to take on hags? We are prepared for low-level orcs and hellhounds, but hags are something only large, well-trained teams expect to take on.

Tigress knelt down and examined the tracks. "I don't like it. I'm guessing a horse drawn cart came through here. There are also some sweeping tracks I can't identify."

Chawett knelt next to Tigress. "These tracks belong to something demonic, or possibly undead. I would say hag, but it wouldn't make sense for them to be on this side of the mountains."

Several thick layers of moist, dark green vines covered the opening. I spread them apart to reveal a path leading into darkness. "You could be right Tigress, this entrance is big enough for at least a small horse and cart."

Chawett spread the vines using his shillelagh. "With the exception of the possibility hags are in here, I love it. This is definitely a unique entrance to the Maze. Everyone gather around me, it's time to fortify our defenses."

Chawett rubbed his hands together creating a small soapy bubble. He then stretched his arms out wide shaping the bubble larger, and larger. "Come quick, we all need to be inside the protection bubble before it pops." He stepped inside.

Tigress slowly stepped into it flashing a brilliant smile. "This is astonishing. How effective is your protection spell?"

"My shield spell would be rated at the enchanter level," Chawett said. "I guarantee it's more than good enough for the one day we'll be in the Maze. As long as you're within my eyesight Tigress, this spell will protect you in many ways."

The more I saw Chawett work, the more I knew we made the right decision. He'd already well-earned his fifth of the treasure.

Chaz stepped into the bubble. "It sure better protect. This is where you earn your keep Mr. magic user."

Dread and I followed Chaz in. The spell's effects could be felt immediately. "Whoa, I'm lighter on my feet and my sword…my sword feels lighter too. This is great!"

"Take a few deep breaths," Chawett instructed. "This spell will give you an energizing high, but don't make the mistake of thinking it'll make you invincible. The shield affects everyone different, in general your reactions will be quicker, fatigue will set in slower, and your body will heal faster. I've even seen hostile projectiles deflect off of those who are highly susceptible to the magic."

The bubble popped with a slight splash.

Dread jumped up and down a few times, clapped his hands, and cracked his knuckles. "Yae-e-yae! That's just what I needed, let's go stack up some gold right now."

We descended into the service entrance in the classic six-man questing team battle formation. Chaz and I were on the front sides, both with swords drawn. Tigress was in-between us with Mustela riding her shoulder on high alert. Dread and Chawett brought up the rear with torches.

We were here. In the Maze. At last.

Though I'd never been here before, it already felt like home-well, a home full of monsters, traps, and darkness. But most of all, gold.

I…was a quester.

CHAPTER 19

I ran my hand along the beaten earth wall, and breathed in the mist. An occasional bat flew over our heads, and rats scurried in the shadows. We followed the twisty, and continuously downward sloping tunnel until it leveled off at an alcove where we stopped to examine the area.

Dread walked around a small abandoned cart. "It's in good order, weird harness though."

"It's official then," Chawett said. "Someone is still bringing supplies in through this tunnel. We need to stay alert."

"Over here." Tigress stared at a portion of wall. "There's a plaque with Talhoffer's crest."

"That plaque can be found at all level one entrances to the Maze." Chawett waved it away and turned back to the abandoned cart. "It says *'A good man out of the good treasure of the heart brings forth good things: and an evil man out of the evil treasure brings forth evil things'*. These next few steps put us in a deadly game team, I can smell the sweet stench of orc urine already."

Tigress sniffed the stale air. "It does smell bad down here, what type of orcs do you think they are?"

"Orcs on the first three or four levels tend to be small, unskilled, and lightly armed," Chawett said. "They travel in groups of at least five though, and can be stupidly fearless. The deeper into the Maze you get, the tougher the orcs are. You wouldn't want to be caught more than six levels deep without a minimum fifteen man questing team."

We stepped down a flight of steep dirt steps. At the bottom our surroundings changed from earthen tunnel, to a smooth, manmade walled hallway. The smell of smoke, and rancid meat wafted in a slight draft.

I gripped my sword tighter than ever before. My heart galloped. I was only eight when I heard my first story of the Maze. That bloodied magic user told me all about the perilous job of questing. When I told him I had no magic, he said that didn't matter. *"Just learn to swing a sword"* was what he said. He then dropped a gold coin in my palm, got mobbed by pretty women, and purchased a case of honey wine. I learned to swing a sword, and now finally…I was in the Cave Maze.

We continued forward until we stood at a three-way intersection, the first turning point on the map. The corridor ahead led into darkness. The other two paths had a yellow glow further down.

I stopped and backed the team up. "These halls are lit."

Chawett looked down both corridors. "Most fruitful areas of the Maze are lit by wall torches. The orcs light them, it's a sure sign they're near."

I ran the tip of my sword across the wall to watch it spark. These walls are as real as can be, and my sword is solid. "Right turn here."

Dread peeked around the corner and gave the hall a long stare. "What about hags? Is there any sign of hags down there?"

Chaz took a step down the hall, bent his knees, and pointed his sword forward. "Chawett said orcs Dread, now lets go take them for everything they have got."

"Douse the torches team," I say. "It's time to run the gauntlet."

We took careful steps down the hall. Soon we came to a point where two large wooden doors paralleled each other.

I turned to the door on the right. "This is the first room the map indicates to be packing possible treasure. I hear some commotion in there."

Chaz gently kicked the bottom of the left door. "This one is already open a crack. There's no commotion this way, I'm going in."

"Wait—" I started to object but Tigress and Dread were all ready in the door behind him.

Chawett nodded his head my way and walked in. "Come on Raff, this looks safe enough."

I came in behind them. Dying candles dimly light the front of this small square room. We all gathered at its unusual centerpiece.

Three waist-high glass cubes sat in a line. The one on the left had several black rats-did they have Talhoffer's toxic fleas on them yet? They scurried and fought each other for position in the overcrowded cage. The middle one had thick white smoke curling inside, and five small brown sacks sitting on top. The one to the right contained a massive swarm of fleas. Tubes with trap doors connected the cubes together.

"This is what Talhoffer does," Chawett said. "What you got here is the makings of some torturous quester trap. We should leave."

Dread grabbed one of the five sacks and stuck his nose in it. "I think these sacks contain huo-yao, and a lot of it." He stuffed each sack into the heavynessless bag.

"I see you Dread," Chaz lifted his chin. "I am keeping a mental note of everything you put in our little bag."

"Good." Dread put his hands on either side of the middle cube and looked closely into it. "This is at least partially huo-yao smoke. I can see a solitary rat in here too."

Clunk! The rat sprung against the glass in a failed attempt to bite Dread. It was sickly skinny with puss-oozing buboes larger than its head. The rat spat blood then keeled over dead. A swarm of fleas jumped off its body and slammed against the glass in our direction.

Dread backed away. "Like Chawett said, we should leave."

"Thank you," I said. "The door across the hall is the one outlined on the map."

Tigress yelped and hopped into my arms. "Rats, I hear them. On the floor."

"Not rats." I set her down, feeling not an ounce of attraction. Funny how quickly that changed. "It's something else."

I took down a candle and scanned the floor in the direction of the noise. I ran into six round top cages at the bottom of the back wall, all contained pixies. The one in the cage closest to me had a tear in its wing, but still managed to fly to the bars. It was filthy, and had a long frown on its tiny face.

Tigress joined me in looking at them. "I have always heard they are happy, magical little pranksters. These look so sad."

Chaz rattled the top of a cage. "We could make a lot of gold selling these little pigeons. Dead or alive they are worth a lot."

I cut the glowing string that latched the cage door and whispered inside. "Porridge sent me, tell her I said hello." The pixie climbed out of the cage and flew across the room. "Help me open the cages—"

Tigress sheathed her daggers. "Already done."

The pixies took to the air and exited the room with a quiet flutter.

Chaz tried to swat the last one but missed. "Pesky little gnats. They will probably alert the hags of our whereabouts."

Chawett stood at the door. "Pixies do not associate with—" He closed his eyes and blew out a breath. "Lets just get out of this room."

Back in the corridor Chawett held his ear to our original target door. "I can recognize that butt-ugly language in there anywhere. That's orcish chatter."

Dread got up close to the door handle and prodded the locking mechanism with his finger.

"How long to pick the lock?" I asked.

"Conveniently it's unlocked," Dread said. "We should be able to get the drop on whatever's in here."

Chaz, Dread, and I readied our swords and took the front. Chawett and Tigress brought up the rear. Tigress pulled back an arrow in ready to fire position. Chawett rubbed his hands together and took up an on-guard stance.

My heart thumped madly. My first Maze battle. Let me in there. I gently pushed Tigress bow down. "Why don't you go in with your daggers? That head slicing move you made on the troll was eye-popping."

Dread nodded vigorously. "Daggers Tigress, please."

Tigress' eyes narrowed. "I'm good smartasses. One shoot with my bow, then I'll jump in with the daggers. It worked against the troll."

Dread's eyes bulged. "But you missed the troll. We're looking at close quarter, hand-to-hand combat here. Now put the bow away."

Tigress drew back her bow and penetrated the door with her eyes. "I *will* not. I am half elf, and I *will* kill something with this bow on this run."

Chawett waved his hand. "Enough talk. Orcs are on the other side of that door. You need to be ready for the fight of your life. Kill or be killed, dragged, raped, and eaten by these savages. There are no do-overs here, so be faultless with what ever attack you choose."

Drops of sweat ran down the side of my face. All the stories of orc battles and now I was here. This would be my first door in the Maze, an encounter I was sure to never forget lay behind it. "We're going in on the count of three. One, two, three."

⚔ CHAPTER 20 ⚔

We busted in the room. Chaz and Dread rushed three small pitchfork-wielding orcs on the right side of the room. I was unlucky. The orc in front of me was a giant, greasy beast three times bigger then the other ones. He held a meat cleaver in his hand, covered in blood. A slaughtered horse lay at his feet.

I ran up on my orc and uppercut with my sword. My intention was to end this quick by slicing him in two. He turned from his butcher job just in time to block my sword with his cleaver. Sparks flew and the clank shuttered through my body. The orc kicked me in the chest sending me sliding back across the floor to the door. Chawett and Tigress took up positions around me.

"This guy is going to take a team effort," I said. "Feel free to jump in."

The orc butcher let out a chunk-splattering belch and lumbered toward the three of us. He swung the massive cleaver in a blurry fast side-to-side figure eight motion.

Chawett's fingernail glowed blue, he pointed to an ox-sized mystery meat carcass that hung from a nearby hook. "Time to make this a food fight."

Whipping his finger to the right, the carcass flung across the room and slammed upside the butcher's head. The orc stumbled sideways, flipped, and disappeared over the wall of a flame spitting fire pit.

Chawett then rapid fire whipped his finger causing four smaller carcasses to smash the orcs engaged with Chaz and Dread.

One flabby meat hunk smacked, then wrapped around an orc's head getting lodged into its spiked helmet. Blinded, the orc spun in a circle trying to rip it off. Chaz sliced the spinning target up with three quick strokes. He looked down at his kill, tasted the air with his tongue and clenched his teeth. "I wish my brother could see this."

Another orc got punched directly in the stomach with a meaty hunk. He doubled over and blew a saucy black puke. Dread swooped in and plunged his sword deep into the back of its head. "Shumminina!"

The final orc dodged one carcass, but got caught by another in the leg. He stumbled forward and hurled his meat fork at Tigress, who had just launched an arrow at him. The two flying objects crossed paths, the arrow logged into the orc's forehead, while Chawett blocked the meat fork with his shillelagh.

Tigress looked at Chawett from the corner of her eye. "Nice reflexes." She then took a few steps toward her victim and arched a sly brow. "What do you think of that arrow placement Dread?"

Dread stood over the dead orc. "Not quite center forehead, it's a little off to the side." He looked at Tigress and smiled. "Nice shooting Tigress."

Chawett took a deep sniff of the air. "Aaaa, the scent of fresh Cave Maze carnage always turns me on. Congratulations on your first Cave Maze victory team Beeston." He picked up the hurled meat fork and examined the tip. "Just don't think it's always this easy, these were not warrior orcs, they were cooks."

Now that the fight settled, I took in my surroundings. A fire pit sat in the middle of the square stone room. The air was chilled, but my battle sweat combatted the cold. I turned the hand crank on a giant rotisserie-spit rod above the main fire pit. "This thing is primed for its next victim."

"I was up next for that rotisserie," says a shaky voice. We spun around. A scruffy man with a dirty gray beard peeked his head from around a back room corner. "Thank you for showing up when you did. My name is Asellus, can you all please help out of these chains?"

Asellus slowly trotted from around the corner. He had the head and torso of a man, with the body of a horse. He was skinny and almost fell when the heavy chains around his legs abruptly stopped him.

"My name is Raff Orcslaughter," I said. "Odd to see a centaur in the Maze. Quite far away from the hidden glens aren't you?"

"That's no centaur," Chaz said. "That's an *ass*-centaur—part donkey, not horse."

"Onocentaur is the preferred, and proper name for my species," Asellus said. "That big orc with the cleaver killed my associate. We were hired by some hags to haul in supplies. Once we delivered, the ghastly whores turned us over to these ignoramuses. That's how I ended up here. Now can you please get me out of these chains?"

Dread examined the shackles near Asellus' hooves. "I just might be able to pick these locks. But first tell me, what was it you hauled in for those hags?"

Asellus scratched his ear and looked around the room. "The load was covered up, and hags don't like questions. I got a peek of the front part of it though. There were a few big chests, most likely filled with gold. The rest smelt of pixies and huo-yao. If you let me out of these chains, I'll tell you where I dropped it. I'm sure you will find something valuable there. I'm no quester, I just want out of this damn place."

Dread easily opened the locks freeing Asellus. The ass-centaur drew directions on the sooty floor with a stick. The hag's drop point was not far away from this room, but out of the boundaries of our map. We all gathered around to look at the crude directions.

"My father said not to go off the map," I said. "I think we should just stay with our original plan, and go to the other four rooms. Lets not forget the rat-flea incident."

Chaz looked at me with wide-eyes. "This information is a gift I refuse to pass up. I have sunk a whole lot of gold into this venture, and so far all we have done has came up with those dumb sacks that better contain huo-yao. Take the room we are in for example, it is the first one on your father's map, and it is a bust. This is a kitchen, not a treasure room. What do we have to look forward to next? Talhoffer's garderobe privy? I'm sure we will find some whiffy treasure for *you* their Raff."

Chaz squatted down to get a better look at Asellus' directions. "Those hags brought in treasure chests, and this could be my only opportunity to turn a profit from this run."

Dread studied the drawing. "I agree with Chaz, those hags must have brought in something valuable."

Chaz's and Dread's opinions were no use when more gold is involved. Frankly, I didn't want another encounter with a hag. I turned to Tigress and Chawett.

Tigress paced the room. "I agree too. We came for gold, and there doesn't seem to be any in this room. I will not be able to purchase a new breeding sniffer with the items in here. What do you think Chawett?"

"I really don't wont to get into a fight with any hags on this run," he said. "They have some ethereal spells that can really mess you up. Asellus, exactly how many hags were with that load?"

"Just four," he said.

Just four? *Just* four? Did my team understand what a hag could do? But maybe I was being a coward. After all, it had been only me against the one hag in Trosworth. This time there were five of us, armed.

"After we dropped the load they took us here where we were supposed to get paid. If you ask me they were on their way out of the Maze. I hope you all do run into those double-crossing witches and kill them."

"Let's hit the four rooms we planned to first," I say. "We can save the hag load mystery room as a last resort, if we don't come up on gold in the planned rooms."

Asellus scratched the ground with his front hoof. "Treasure

doesn't wait for no one in the Maze. If I was you I would not hesitate. But I'm not you. I just want to get out of here. Now if you don't mind I'm going to grab me a snort before I stampede out of this hellhole. These orcs got a wine and ale cabinet nestled here in the back."

"I can use a drink myself," I said. "Lead the way, we both deserve a snort after dealing with those orcs."

Asellus turned the corner. "Have you had a prosperous run thus far?"

"I just came up on five sacks of huo-yao. Gold of course is what were really after."

Asellus opened a thrashed wooden cabinet. One of the rotted doors broke off the hinges and fell to the floor. I reached to pick it up and got bucked in the groin by the ass's two aft hooves. "Arghh!" I fell to the ground on my hands and knees.

Asellus snatched a small treasure chest from the shelf and galloped for the door.

I crawled forward in pursuit, but collapsed just as I got around the corner. "Stop that ass!"

Chawett dropped to a knee, and stretched out his shillelagh.

"Heee-Haw!" Asellus tripped over it sending his face grinding into the floor. The chest tumbled into a wall and smashed open. Dozens of gold coins spun out of it in all directions.

The pain in my groin eased slightly with the sight-My dad was right about gold being in this room.

Asellus got up and hobbled out the door empty-handed.

Chaz shook his head while picking up coins. "See what happens when you help somebody, Raff?"

Tigress helped me up. "You get kicked in the balls. That looked like it hurt."

"I think I see the light Tigress," I said. "I think I see the light."

The team gathered up gold from around the room while I tried to recover from the low blow. Dread added our proceeds to the heavynessless bag then gripped it firmly in his fist. "That still only makes our total sixty-nine gold." He tossed the bag over to me.

I caught it in one hand and then bounced it up and down. "Don't fret, we still got *four* more stops laid out on the map." I tossed the bag over to Chawett.

Chaz intercepted the bag and held it up by the drawstrings. "We have *five* more stops. Let's not forget about the hag's load. Heavynessless or not, this bag is still extremely light."

Chawett snatched the bag away from Chaz, and flung it back to Dread. "To the next room we go."

Dread and I were the last out of the orc's kitchen. The pain from the hoofing slowed me, but I wasn't going to let Chaz see me struggle.

As we exited, Dread paused at a rotisserie-spit rod lined with several unidentified golden brown fowl. "Looks like dinner was almost ready." He snatched a leg off one of the birds and took a bite. "That orc chef knew what he was doing, tastes like chicken."

I was a little hungry, and this actually did smell normal enough. I reached to grab a leg but stopped when I saw something swimming in the sauce bucket near my feet. "What do orcs baste their meat with?"

"I have no idea," Dread said. "But this leg is scrumptious."

I gave the basting brush a stir and tried to lift it up. A pair of eyes peeked out of the dark brown mixture. A slimy tentacle then wrapped around the brush handle and yanked it back down out of my hand.

"I'm going to pass on this gourmet meal. That dodo is going to make you sick cousin."

We left the room and continued down the corridor where we stopped at another three-way intersection. On the left, a hall lead to the supposed hag's load. The path straight ahead was where stop number three on the map is. To the right, a large set of wooden double doors.

"There you go Dread," I said. "What do you think lies behind door number two?"

Dread sucked all remaining meat off the now glistening 'chicken' bone and flung it back down the hallway. He then wiped his mouth off on his sleeve and licked his fingertips. "Let me at it."

He pulled a tiny ear trumpet from his tool kit and held it to the doors. "I don't hear anything going on inside, but these doors are thick, I can't be sure. There's no lock, all we need to do is come on in." He grabbed the handles and pushed with no results. "It seems to be wedged shut, or maybe locked from behind."

"Let me try." I pushed on the doors but they did not budge.

Dread reached for a chest-buster. "I can blast this door down if we need to."

"If it's unlocked we're not wasting a chest-buster on it," I said. "There's more than enough room for all five of us to push. Let's do it team."

"Heave!" We all pushed on the doors at the same time. There was a cracking sound, and dirt fell from the upper jamb onto our heads.

"Heave!" The doors flung open, we all fell in a dusty smoke filled pile on the other side. I look up to see twenty plus orcs staring at us from two oversized dinner tables. "Run!"

Chaz popped off the pile and sprinted away first. He ran straight down the hag load hallway. Tigress followed helping Chawett along with his gear. Dread and I struggled up off the bottom. We both grabbed a handle and slammed the doors shut. We then ran full speed to catch up with the rest of the team. The ground shook beneath our feet as the orc horde slammed into the doors from the other side.

We caught up to Chawett and Tigress at the end of the hall where it turned to the left. There was a long stretch there with over twenty doors evenly spaced per side. Chaz held open the thirteenth door on the right-the door Asellus identified as having the hags' load.

"Come quick," Chaz said. "This way!"

THE DINNER PARTY

CHAPTER 21

I looked back to see the orcs' doors bust open. The whole dinner party stormed toward us. It was now or never-at least our curiosity would be satisfied.

"To the door then," I said. "Quick!"

We all slid into a small, empty, rectangle shaped room. Chaz quietly closed the door leaving us with just the light coming from underneath it. Chawett jammed his shillelagh between the floor and the bottom of the door, the rest of us barricaded up against it with the full weight of our bodies.

We could hear doors opening, and slamming shut one by one, as the orcs got closer.

Mustela let out a quiet 'chirp' then ducked under Tigress' hair.

Tigress put her lips against my ear. "Mustela's nose isn't completely broken. That chirp is an alarm indicating a trap door—"

Click! The floor swung open from both sides. We all fell straight down. My head banged against the sidewall as I tumbled through the air, dazed. Chawett's fingernail glowed brightly blue.

"We gonna die!" Dreads voice echoed around us. "Ohhh this is it!"

I braced myself for impact when the fall slowed in mid-air. Tigress and Mustela plopped down next to me with a slight bounce. Only we weren't on the ground. We were still falling.

"What is this?" Tigress asked. "What's happening?"

Chaz and Dread slid into us. I felt beneath me and realized what was going on-we were riding this fall out in Chawett's shield bubble.

We hit the ground in a tangled dog pile. The misty spray of the shield bubble splashed over us when the spell broke. The magic slowed our fall, but the landing was still painful. Lucky for us we ended up in what felt-and smelled-like a semi-soft trash heap.

Various grunts, groans, and moans could be heard in the room. A single door across from me was cracked open slightly. A faint flicker of light came in from the outside.

"My leg." Dread clutched his calf, tight. "Oh, I think my leg is broken. But I'm not dead. Is everyone else still alive?"

"My head is pounding," I said. "But I'm good. We must have fallen ten levels deep."

Chawett coughed and hacked. "More like thirteen or fourteen levels deep. If this shaft were any deeper the bubble would have burst sending us all to certain death. Now can somebody thank me by helping me up out of this?"

"I think I can get to you," I said. "Hold tight." I trudged through floor clutter and reached for what looked like Chawett's extended hand. "Are you all right?" Our hands met, his was red hot and crusty. I instinctively let go. Chawett fell back down into the pile. "There's something alive on your hand, it's moving too!"

Chawett held up his hand catching the light. "Son of a wench. I burned up five of my fingers! Aaagh! It feels like my hand was dipped in acid."

I reached out for his good hand and helped him up. He stood using his shillelagh for support.

Chawett glared at his frying hand. "I used every bit of my spell power to sustain that shield bubble." He shook his hand vigorously and blew on it several times. "I can't believe this happened, not just one, but it took *five* of my fingers to pull that off. All five." His voice sank with a threat of tears.

Tigress briefly stood up but slipped back down into the mound of junk. "What is this place?" She picked up a rotted wooden shield from the crud. "The smell in here is putrid. Chaz, what's that on your head?"

Chaz ended up face down in what looked like slightly muddy linen. When he hoisted himself up some of the fabric was pasted across his face and head.

Chaz peeled the object off. He then began spitting, and gagged. "Inhumanity!"

"What is it?" Tigress asked.

"Feces!" Chaz gasped. "These are some foul creature's under garments."

"Quiet down," Chawett said. "I recognize the markings on that shield Tigress. That belongs to an orc sector captain, the type of orc you would find this deep in the Maze."

Dread sat up, smiled, and pointed at Chaz. "Ha Ha. You got a mouth full of sweaty orc ass Chaz. You know that loincloth had some diseased parasites marinating up in it. And you had that nastyness in your mouth."

Chaz slung the specimen in Dread's direction.

"Not today." Dread put his injured leg in hand and rolled sideways to avoid the foul linen.

"Stop playing, you two," I said. "Did you hear what Chawett said? We're in an orc sector captain's closet fourteen levels deep in the Maze."

"I heard him," Chaz said. "We also got a lame thief, a no-nose sniffer, and a spent magic user with no spell power. I understand that this can't get any worse."

I made my way over to the door and looked through the crack. A dying oil lamp lit a huge muscle bound orc sprawled out on a crudely constructed hammock. The brute swung low due to his mass. The stressed bed looked ready to burst. The orc snored and snorted loudly through the grotesque snotty snout that orcs were known for. A cache of weapons hung on the wall behind him, including a heavy-duty battleaxe, and a few rusty longswords.

The room had two closed doors, one at either end. The door on the right had a small open peek hatch. Through it, clanking cups, and vivacious conversation could be heard.

"I got something to say about that 'can't get any worse' statement Chaz," I said. "The grimy slob of an orc whose closet we're in is passed out in there."

Dread hobbled over to the door, knelt down, and peeked through the crack below me. "He still has a half empty bottle of wine in hand, and I sure am thirsty. It looks like there are some potential valuables on the shelf above his head too. I see a stack of at least thirty gold coins on the left, a mystery box in the middle, and-bless his heart-that sure looks like a mini bottle of Chugalug's sparkling green fairy on the right. I'm going to get it all."

Tigress wedged her way between us to view the room. "That's no mystery box Dread. That's one of Talhoffer's personal treasure boxes. It looks just like the one above the bar at King Heads."

Dread shot up. "Really?"

Chaz barged his head through us. "Let me see. Yes, yes that's undoubtedly one of Talhoffer's treasure boxes. Our fortunes have officially changed, we must have it."

Chawett peered through the crack from one knee. "Agreed, but we don't want to wake up that orc, he's definitely a captain, and we're in no shape to take him on. Do you see that knotted rope hanging from the ceiling by his bed? If he pulls it we'll have to contend with his unruly clan of drunken guards in the other room."

I pushed on the door. It creaked a little but the orc didn't move. "Well we don't want to be in this closet when the captain comes for his loin cloth. Let's make this theft quick. Dread, can you grab the goods with your bum leg?"

"Raff, when treasure's involved, nothing could stop me."

That was my cousin. A bad leg wouldn't make him flinch. Not

when there was gold, and green fairy in the balance. "We'll wait for you at the door on the other side of the room."

Dread dropped back down to a knee and studied the area. "The box looks heavy. I don't think I'll be able to lift it without standing directly on that monster's greasy forehead. I can sneak up from the side, lift the box open, and take the item out though. That is if my leg cooperates, it's a little tender."

"What happened to *"nothing could stop me"*?" I ask.

Tigress poked Dread's leg. "I saw the way you shot up when you heard that was one of Talhoffer's boxes. Stop being such a big baby."

"It's like magic," he said. " Seeing Talhoffer's box made my leg all better, or maybe it's just a strain."

"Well that's the plan then," I said. "Be quiet as a mouse, the fat cat is near."

We tiptoed to the door at the far end of the room and carefully opened it. I gave Dread a thumb up-time for him to do what he did best.

Hobbling alongside the wall, Dread crept his way toward the shelf. He gently closed the peek hatch when passing the guardroom door, and then studied himself at the orc's bedside. Smiling, he gave me a wink when snatching the easily accessible bottle of green fairy. He stuffed it into the heavynessless bag then focused on Talhoffer's box. With his tongue hanging out, Dread balanced on one wobbly foot and leaned over the orc.

Tigress held Mustela tight in her arms. "Steady Dread."

With one hand Dread flipped and held open the box, with the other he pinched the item and flicked it into the heavynessless bag.

I waved for Dread to come back, but his eyes already locked on the teetering stack of gold coins. He pulled the curved stick from his belt and stretched it out toward the far end of the shelf.

Chawett crowded the door. "Dread's using the butt scratcher to reach the gold."

Fully extended, Dread was just able to reach the valuable gold coin tower. Then, hovering dangerously above the orc, he slowly started dragging the stack his way with the stick. A clump of displaced dust floated down to the heavy snoring orc's nostrils.

"Haahh-haahh-ACHOO!" The orc made a savage turn in the hammock, dropping his bottle of booze to the floor.

Dread swept the gold into the bag, snatched up the fallen bottle, and fast-hobbled for the open door.

After he whisked by me I took a last look at the orc. He was still passed out cold. I closed the door and breathed a sigh as I leaned against it on the other side.

Dread gulped down of the remainder of the orc's wine then smashed the bottle down to the floor. "Aaaaa, this guy had the good stuff." He pounded his chest three times and squinted. "That's a harsh burn right there."

I held my ear to the door. "Did you have to smash the bottle? Nobody wants to fight that big ugly thing in there."

Dread stood slack-mouthed. "Let a thief celebrate a taste. I just stole one of Talhoffer's personal treasures from an orc sector captain's bedroom. While he was in it. It's called master thievery."

Chaz strode over to Dread's side. "Well done thief. Lets have a look at that Talhoffer item. What was that in the box?"

Dread stuck his hand into the bag, felt around, and then pulled out a simple gold ring engraved with Talhoffer's crest. We all surrounded Dread to get a good look at the prize.

Chawett gawked. "That's Talhoffer's Gold Ring of Enhanced Wizardry."

"What are its powers?" Tigress asked.

"On a normal man's finger it has no power," Chawett said. "But on the finger of a magic user it means everything. That ring will take even a lowly magician to the level of wizard instantaneously. With the added power of Talhoffer's ring I would be the most highly sought after magic user in all of Broxington."

Chaz cleared his throat. "Uuummm, yeaaah, that's not going happen. The ring will be put up for sale to the highest bidder. Let me get a closer look at that."

Dread hesitantly handed Chaz the ring.

Chaz put it on his finger and made a fist. "There have got to be magic users out there willing to pay upwards of a few thousand gold coins for this."

"Why can't Chawett use it until we get out of the Maze?" I ask.

"Yeah." Tigress lifted Mustela to her shoulder. "That ring won't do us any good if we don't get out of here alive."

Chaz acted as though he didn't hear. Now wasn't the time to pry it off his hand. We needed to escape. "Chawett, do you recognize this place?"

Ahead of us stretched a long hallway with a stone floor. I could barely make out a door just like the one we came through all the way down at the other end. In the middle of the hall stood a vestibule with double doors to the left, and a bench facing it to the right.

"This is the longest hallway I have ever seen in the Maze," Chawett said. "I've definitely never run into anything like this before, but then again, I've never been in this deep."

Tigress started walking ahead of us. "Lets go before that orc realizes his ring and wine are gone. Drinking in the Maze is foolish." She glared at Dread.

He stumbled. "What Tigress? I deserve a little something after securing our payday. There was really only a swallow in the container. It made my leg feel better. I'm injured, remember? Chaz, we need you to give Chawett the ring. He might even be able to heal my leg with its power."

Chawett looked down at his hand and spread his fingers. "Full disclosure though." He looked up. "Once I don the ring it magically *cannot* be removed. That's the way it is when magic users wear Talhoffer items." He held his ring finger out toward Chaz. "Lace me with it."

Chaz made a fist, covered it with his other hand, and brought them both into his chest. "That is not true. We can simply have your finger amputated once we get out. That's how we get the ring back."

Chawett dropped his arm down. "Oh I'm not losing another

finger. It's not going down like that."

Bam! A loud thump and deep grunt came from the orc sector captain's room.

"See that?" Chaz started running down the hall. "Your wasting time with all the bickering. Now he's awake! I'll give you the ring down the hall. Let's go before we're discovered."

We all ran to the center of the hall and the vestibule. Chawett took a seat on the bench and tried to catch his breath. Dread and I examined the wrought iron double doors. Three heavy locks lined evenly down the middle.

I gave one of the locks a tug. "Do you have any idea what could be behind this monstrosity, Chawett?"

"A door like this might just access a stairwell out of these depths," he said. "A treasure room, or monster allocation center are also possibilities. Talhoffer is full of surprises when you reach these levels."

Dread pulled a small tool from his kit and began working it into the bottom lock. "No good, it will take me half a day to get all these open."

"Set the chest-busters with the quickness Dread," I said. "Let's hope this is a way out of here, and Chaz, give up the ring all ready!"

Chaz pulled and spun the ring on his finger. "It seams to be stuck."

Dread mounted the explosives and began unraveling the igniter cord. "If you don't pull that ring off you finger in the next three seconds I'm amputating your—"

"Stop taking so long!" Tigress fast walked down the hall. "Let's go for the door at the other end. It's only a matter of time before—"

Boom! The door we had entered in came crashing down. The orc captain stepped into the hall and threw Talhoffer's empty treasure box against the wall, breaking it into pieces. He let out an intense roar and peered down the hall at us.

Chawett faced the orc and rubbed his palms together. "Time to see if I can muster up some five-finger miracle magic power. I just may be able to save this team one more time."

He held out his good hand and smacked it with his palm. A melon sized lava sphere formed, and flickered firelight against the walls of the hall.

The sphere's heat hit the side of my face. "Yes!" He still had power.

The orc captain's hoard of twelve guards rumbled into the hall behind him. With his unit in place the captain led their charge with steady pounding stomps.

Chawett cocked his hand back, took four running steps, and rolled the lava sphere toward our approaching enemies. The sphere grew like a snowball rolling down hill into a tremendous ball of red hell fire.

Three of the orcs turned around and sprinted for the exit squealing. The others stopped in their tracks, knelt down, and raised shields as a wall of defense of the magic.

As the sphere got close to the orcs it lost its fire, turned a cool shade of blue, and shrunk to the size of an egg. It wobbled to a slow stop directly in front of the captain's foot.

The brute stood up, trapped the sphere under his boot, and stepped down to crush the sphere-and our hopes-into the floor. He then burst into laughter and let out a shrieking call. With that, the door at the opposite end of the hall swung open. A pack of hellhounds streamed out of the door. They barked and howled in a bloodthirsty frenzy. The captain then waved on his gang to continue their rabid march.

Chawett spun around to Chaz. "The ring!"

Dread took a quick glance at the wave of oncoming hounds. "Are those crotch masticators?"

"Quick!" I turned to Chaz. "Give Chawett the ring!"

Chaz yanked the heavynessless bag from Dread's belt and backed up to the wall. He drank back a potion and threw the triangle-shaped bottle at my chest-the same style bottle that contained Entry Cave teleportation potion at Moe's. "I guess that skirmish with the troll was worthwhile after all. I knew this potion would come in useful.

Farewell idiots."

A snake-like swirl of light twisted up Chaz's body. In an instant he transported out of the Maze.

PART THREE

"THE SPOILS"

CHAPTER 22

Dread lunged for Chaz but it was to late. "Son of a wench! He got the gold."

"Damn that, cuz!" I said. "Pull the string, bust the door!"

Chawett, Tigress, and I propped up the bench as a barrier against the blow. Dread slid under it and pulled the igniter string. The explosion blew a thick cloud of black smoke our way. Shrapnel whizzed all around us.

"Go, go, go!" I said.

We rushed forward using the bench to ram whatever remained of the doors. Upon contact they burst open. "We're through!"

A few fleeting steps down a short vestibule led to an enormous arena with a giant arched ceiling. We tossed the bench aside and skid to a stop. A monumental battle between a large party of questers and an entire orc tribe filled the corridor. Various groups of questers engaged in vicious weapon-clanking battle all around the arena.

"This just gets better and better!" Dread wrapped his hands around his bum leg.

The robust quester in front of me pulled the spiked end of his battle-axe out of an orc's head then kicked the dead body away. He turned around-questing Captain Castillo Gabbiano.

"What are you people doing here?" Castillo roared.

"We got orcs and hounds coming in hot behind us." I said.

"You got what?" Castillo yelled.

Five hellhounds leaped from the smoky vestibule with fire breath ablaze. Dread and I raised our shields in unison, deflecting two of them off to our left.

The three others cut to our right where they ambushed one of Castillo's team members. The man was entangled with an orc in face-to-face combat when the attack began. The first hound snatched the sniffer smooth off his shoulder and ripped it in half. The other two bit down on his arms and began to shred. When he spun to fight off the hounds, the orc he was entangled with sunk its sword in and up his back.

"Nooooooo!" Castillo swung his axe with a frantic thrust slicing completely through all three of the hounds. He then spun around and sliced his weapon through the orc's neck that killed his team member. "Rearguard to arms!"

Tigress and Chawett took on the two deflected hounds leaving Dread and I standing directly in front of the rushing orc sector captain and his guard. We took our best battle stance and prepared for impact when six of Castillo's men rushed past us and collided with them. They bucked off the Captain and his first two grunts but were swarmed by the preceding orc rank.

Dread and I joined forces with the men giving us the upper hand, and a pile of dead orc scum in no time. The sector captain ended up with the spiked end of Castillo's battle-axe logged directly in his heart.

Our team regrouped and joined in fighting alongside Castillo's team until all the orcs and hounds in the room were slain.

I sheathed my sword, leaned against a wall, and slid down slowly to the floor.

A bloody, stomped-out hound near me had foam bubbling, and smoke smoldering from its mouth. The half-dead animal struggled, but managed to shakily stand on its three remaining legs, then lunge at me.

Dread stomped his foot down in front of the dog. "This won't be no flesh wound, ya three-legged bitch!"

He upper cut the dog's jaw with a speedy swing of his sword. The impact sent the animal up and down with a deadened thud.

"Thanks cousin," I said.

Dread, and Tigress leaned against the wall next to me. Chawett took a knee in front of us and tried to catch his breath. Dead and mangled bodies littered the arena.

Tigress scrunched her lips. "I really hope I can get this horrendous image out of my mind one day. I doubt I will ever forget the smell."

Castillo's team was very well organized. They collected gold, weapons and anything else of value from their victims. After dealing with their dead they made camp. Three fighters stood in a line blocking the darkened East end of the arena.

"Chawett, what do you think is going on behind those men?" I asked. "It looks like Castillo doesn't want anyone over there. I'm going to investigate."

"Not a good idea Raff," he said. "We don't want to get on Castillo's bad side anymore then we all ready are. You do know we need his help to get out of here. We got to work out some kind of deal to tag along with his team on their way to the top. It's the only chance we have to get out of these depths alive."

Tigress dragged her boot across the floor. "But we just killed all the orcs. Let's explore for a while. We might find treasure, and a way out on our own."

"We only killed all the orcs *in this arena*." Chawett pointed to the large arched wooden double doors at the arenas end. "Outside those doors we got at least thirteen level perils to contend with, and a lot of them. I'm talking about vile wandering monsters, heavily armed orc tribes, and of course the undead. Not to mention Talhoffer's worst death traps. Even if we could deal with those things we would be endlessly lost without a map of this area."

"Let's go talk to Castillo now then," I said. "Come on team."

Castillo and several of his men stood in a semi circle. A female thief was in the middle scuffling to open a chest. She worked one of her long, dingy, pick-like fingernails into the lock.

I figured their gathering had something to do with treasure. "Pardon me Sir. Castillo."

He looked up at us briefly then returned his attention to the thief at work. "No, no, no! The third rivet, then yank."

"Sir. Castillo, my name is Raff Orcslaughter and I—"

Castillo clinched his fists and looked at me with bulging eyes. "You sons a bitches got my top thief and only sniffer killed. Bonnaroo was my closest friend, and the best chest opener I have ever quested with. Thanks to you, all I'm left with is this stank, sniveling, non-chest opining runt of a thief you see right here."

The thief turned her head and glared up at Castillo. Her wart-littered face revealed some faint dwarf-like features. A thin stream of yellowish mucus ran from her black-tooth ridden mouth.

Dread could open that chest in half a heartbeat, but I wasn't about to make that common knowledge. Not unless it gained us something.

Castello kicked the thief hard in the back. "Get back to work Gnarly! Your condolences are unwelcome here Raff Orcslaughter. Now get the hell away from my camp."

Chawett stepped up to Castello. "We fell down a pit to these depths and need to join up with your team to get out of the Maze. We'll help fight off anything encountered on the way up."

"And we have a mighty fine thief," I pointed out.

Castillo chuckled mockingly. "Chawett Loinchop, I should have known your half-ass, no magic-casting, rat-soup eating self would be with these non-accredited questers. Hell no! There is no way I would let you fools piggyback on us. You'll just end up getting more of my men killed."

Gnarly yanked her nail and the treasure chest popped open. All eyes turned to the shinny gold immersed in crystal clear water inside.

Castillo motioned to one of his fighters. "Fergus, take this gold and add it to my pile."

Just as Fergus was about to reach both hands in, Dread pushed him aside. He picked up one end of the chest and dumped its entire contents.

Razor-toothed maggots scrambled from the spill searching for victims. Everyone scattered to avoid the chomping pests. Some of the maggots dug into the ground, others were squashed under heavy boots.

After crushing a few of the dangerous maggots Fergus looked at his hands. He then looked at Dread. "Thanks for that, thief. I'd be maggot food if it weren't for you."

Castillo righted the chest and slammed it shut. "Leave my camp! If I catch any of you following us on the way out I will have your whole team murdered. Now go on, get out of here."

Gnarly grunted and kicked dirt at us as we walked away.

Castillo laughed out loud. "That's right Gnarly, get them out of my face!"

We set up camp in the opposite corner of the room from Castillo and his men. Dread broke up the shield bench to use as wood for a fire. We all took a seat around it. The warmth brought the only comfort in this forsaken section of the cave. I tried not to think about everything that just happened.

Tigress cuddled Mustela in her lap. "We need a plan."

Chawett rubbed his hands together in an attempt to create a lava sphere. "Nothing. I've exhausted all my useful spell power. We will be dead long before it regenerates, and that's *if* it regenerates. I'm only a five-finger magic user now."

Dread elevated his leg on a rock and rubbed his knee. "I could really use that bottle of green fairy from the orc captain's room to sooth my leg."

Chawett held up his bad hand and flicked flakes of char off the tips of his nubs. "I've seen a lot of betrayals in this Maze, but what Chaz did was extra ugly. With that ring on my finger we could have fought our way out of just about anything. And then there's the gold, we could have used what little we did have to pay Castillo to take us to the top. Now we have nothing to barter with. And nothing from nothing leaves nothing. Two questers per level deep is the standard survival rule for questing. We're a five-man team in the deepest depths. This is a death sentence."

I did my best to get comfortable on the hard dirt floor. "We've survived everything the Maze has thrown at us so far and overcame some nasty stuff. Lets try and get a little rest. We'll have to come up with an exit strategy before Castillo's team leaves here."

It seemed as if I had just fell asleep when I got a push in the ribs. I jumped up quick to find Gnarly standing directly in front of me.

CHAPTER 23

"Castillo has a proposition for you all," Gnarly squeaked. I put my hand over my mouth and nose to block the foul smell of her tart breath. "Come with me. All of you."

Propositions. I liked propositions, especially when our other options amounted to a big fat zero.

Dread stood next to me and put his finger in Gnarly's face. "Your breath smells like a bucket of rancid ogre armpits Gnarly. You need to go chew on some mint leaves or something."

Gnarly grunted and spun around. "Come with me, a proposition awaits you."

Castillo watched us approach with a crooked smile. "My team member Fergus here came up with an idea that can possibly save your people Raff. He tells me your thief took a few of my team members for quite a bit of gold at the shell game back in Trosworth. It's because of his supposed skill at the game that I am willing to offer you a deal. If he can solve Les Trois Perdants, and provide me with it's prize, we will safely escort your team up to the Entry Cave."

"So Les Trois Perdants really exists," mumbled Dread.

"What exactly *is* Les Trois Perdants?" Tigress scratched Mustela behind the ears.

"I know all about it," Chawett said. "Word is there are three identical treasure chests floating above a bottomless pit. Two chests empty, one loaded with gold. An unstable earthen plank reaches out over the pit with three rocks at the end. Step to the rocks and the chests will shut and shuffle. Once they settle you throw a rock at the chest containing gold. If you hit the correct one it will float down to deliver you its ample bounty."

Castillo laughed. "Throw a rock at the incorrect one and the chests, along with the plank, and yourself, drop into the pit. This is a one-time offer. If you say no, that's it. Once the chests fall they don't reset for over a year, so you will need to make this count. Do we have a deal?"

"Picking the correct chest won't be a problem for Dread," I said. "In addition to the escort out of the Maze we want a fifty-fifty split of the gold. Do we have a deal?"

Castillo's head snapped to the left where he stared unblinking at one of his younger questers. The young man took a slow step back. "Uhh, he actually *did* just say that boss. That man said he wants a fifty-fifty split."

Castillo's head whipped back to me. "There will be absolutely no cut. This was going to be Bonnaroo's job until *you* got him killed. An escort to the mouth of the Entry Cave is *all* I offer. The complete contents of the chest go to me."

"No pay, no play," I said. "We *don't* have a deal." I ignored the glares from my team. Sure, we were desperate, but we weren't going to risk our lives to escape this place with nothing. Dread was the thief. Me? I could haggle 'til all the world's mead dried up.

"Have it your way Raff," Castillo said calmly. "Gnarly! It's time for you to walk the Les Trois Perdants plank."

"We'll take the deal," Dread said. "Show me to the chests."

I ran a hand over my face. Why did Dread have to step in and mess-up our chances for a payout?

"I thought you would see it my way," Castillo said. "Follow me."

We trailed behind Castillo and a contingent of his men. The line of guards followed us toward the dark end of the arena. I gave Dread a shove at his shoulder. "Our team members don't do that free stuff

Dread."

"I know this," he said. "But we have no choice. Chawett, what more do I need to know about the Perdants?"

"I've never heard of any quester picking correctly," Chawett said. "Are you sure about doing this? You got the part about a bottomless pit right?"

Dread clapped his hands. "I've seen Bonnaroo do his thing at the shell game before. He was very good, but I'm better than him. If Bonnaroo thought he could do this, then I know I can."

"Light up my nemesis!" Castillo bellowed out.

Fighters on either end of the room dipped their torches into large circular pits. Flames erupted lighting the area.

Three large chests bobbled slightly in mid air. A blinding yellow glow resonated from the shimmering treasure stashed in the middle one.

Tigress' mouth dropped "Wow, there has got to be over ten thousand gold coins in that thing."

I grit my teeth. Ten thousand gold coins that would all go to Castillo.

Castillo and his men took up positions along the pits edge. Dread stood at where the plank began and surveyed the area. He then sauntered up it to the three rocks at the end. At once, all three chests slammed shut.

Tigress took my hand and squeezed tight. "You can do it Dread."

The gold-bearing chest slowly switched places with the chest on the right. After a brief pause, it circled over and switched with the chest on the far left and stopped.

"My gold says he's in the pit," hollered one of Castillo's men.

"I like the cut of the thief's jib," said another. "I'm taking all bets!" He got mobbed with takers.

Dread did not take his eyes off the chests. He nodded and made a hand gesture for everyone to be quiet. The chests whipped around each other. They spun faster and faster in a confusing switching flurry. Slowly they came to a stop.

After a moment of silence one of Castillo's men yelled out. "It's the chest on the right!"

"No, no, no!" Another man yelled. "It's the middle chest! The middle chest is the one!"

Tigress bounced up and down. "Witch one do you think has the gold Raff?"

"I couldn't tell you," I said. "They were moving stupidly fast."

The plank started to shake slightly as Dread contemplated our fate.

"Study long, study wrong!" a quester squawked. "Come on thief! Pick a chest!"

Castillo waved his hands in a panic. "Throw a rock before the plank breaks up you fool! Do something now!"

Dread picked up a rock and threw it at the chest on the right, it popped open upon impact to reveal the gold.

"He chose correct!" I said.

Dread turned around sporting a huge smile. "Yah that! I'm the king at this game!" The chest slammed shut behind him.

Dread slipped to one knee nearly falling off the plank. His head spun back around to the chest. "What's this?"

The chests once again began to shuffle.

"That's a good start thief," Castillo hollered. "You got to choose correct three times to get the prize!"

Thick frosty white snow flurries steamed up from the pit. The arena's temperature instantly dropped to a shivering cold.

I stepped to the pit's edge and peered into the confusion. "Now that's just foul. Talhoffer is way dirty for that right there. I can hardly see a thing."

The chests spun around each other this time faster than before. The motion created a furious twisting blizzard in the freezing steam. The whole mess looked like a swirling white and brown tornado of chaos. Once again the chests slowed to a stop. The plank buckled down a notch and started shaking.

Dread snatched up the second rock. "Sometimes you got to let your nuts hang!" He threw the rock toward the chest on the left. It got hit and sprung open to once again reveal the gold.

"That's my cousin!" I yell. "One more time Dread. You can do it."

The chest closed and began to shuffle with the others. They spun and moved up and down in a lightning fast crisscross pattern. The room dropped further in temperature. Condensation below Dread's feet began to freeze turning it into an ice sheet. He slipped around, but didn't take his eyes off the chests.

"This is it!" Castillo yelled. "Be quick, that plank won't be under your feet for much longer."

As soon as the chests came to a stop the plank cracked. Dread reached for the final stone but it popped away and slid backward down the icy shuddering plank. Dread dived for the stone, picked it up on the slide, and sent it zinging toward the chests. The projectile ricocheted off the top right corner of the middle chest then popped up in a high arch before landing on top of the chest on the right. The snow flurries then blasted the pit so thick they engulfed all the chests into a white out. The whole arena began to rumble.

Dread slid out of the fog. The plank collapsed behind him with a crash down into the pit. "Did I hit the right one?"

"You hit two different ones," I said. "I can't see what the chests are doing through all that fog."

"What's happening up there?" Castillo yelled. "Did he hit the correct chest? Somebody answer me!"

Several of Castillo's questers leaned over the pit's edge trying to confirm the outcome. The entire arena suddenly took a deep drop then bounced and tilted. I fell to all fours on instinct, flattening myself against the ground. Two of Castillos questers fell into the pit. Several other men got knocked down and slid into walls. Others ran to the back of the arena in search of stable ground.

Chawett and Tigress were close enough to the walls that the tilt didn't affect them much.

Dread tried to stand up but fell in the shaking. "Did I choose right? Did I?"

Castillo stood firm through the rumble. He looked steadfast into the air above the pit. The shaking stopped and a chest soared out of the mist. It slammed down and spilt a flowing tsunami of gold coins across the ground.

Castillo ran to the spillage, dropped to his knees, and cascaded the gold through his fingers. "Ha, ha, haaaa! You bootless questers have officially acquired an escort out of the Maze!"

Tigress ran into Dread giving him a big hug. "You did it!"

Mustela pranced from Tigress's shoulder onto Dread's, swirled around his neck and dooked.

My desire for the gold didn't hold a candle to my relief at Dread's safety.

Dread dusted himself off and wiped the sweat from his brow. "Nothing to it family, you already know the shell game is what I do."

A Chest

CHAPTER 24

We packed our things and took a position at the rear of Castillo's team. After traveling up five winding levels we came to a stop.

Fergus came sliding backward across the ground.

A quester ran up on him with balled up fists. He stared down Fergus with one eye, the other wondered upward. "Why the hell do I have to wear a blindfold? I just killed three orcs, and took a scorching hounds bite in the ass for that man. As a matter of fact this is my third run in with Castillo. I can be trusted!" He spat on the ground in our direction. "You can't treat me like these losers."

Castillo appeared behind the man, grabbed a wall torch, and clubbed him in the back of the head. He dropped to the ground and rolled, trying to knock burning embers from his hair. "Your ass not the only thing scorching is it Cockeye? Blindfold this fool before he gets left behind. And double blind fold team Beeston here."

A short walk later I heard what sounded like a large stone being moved. Then, still blindfolded, we ascended a tight spiral staircase at least three levels, maybe four. I attempted to count the turns, rises, and switchbacks, but my memory didn't cooperate. Besides, it'd be a long time before I wanted to descend to level thirteen again.

Once again I heard the sound of a large stone being moved. A short walk later the blindfolds are removed. Five more levels of confusing twists and turns had us out of the main entry cave, the sun directly overhead.

Blindfolds were removed.

Noon. I'd almost forgotten the luxury of sunlight. Tall trees surrounded us, breaking only to allow a dusty trail to lead to the Maze entrance. I took a deep breath. "The fresh air of Broxington's Light Woods has never smelt so good."

"It don't smell that good to me," Dread said. "By my calculations we are two days away from Beeston. That puts us one day behind our deadline with Joe. Not that it matters, we have no huo-yao, and no gold to buy any."

After what we'd just been through, a run-in with Joe didn't intimidate me one bit. We followed Castillo's team down the Elfin Toll Road to the point of toll collection. A stone arch spans the road where several elf's stand guard. From the back of the procession I watch some negotiating between Castillo and the elf leader. Without looking back Castillo gave a wave to proceed, and walked off with the elf leader laughing loudly.

As we approach the arch an elf advanced on us with a few of his band. He looked us over then spoke with Tigress in a notably grumpy version of the elfin language.

"We have a problem," Tigress said. "The elves require payment for us to continue down their road. When I told him we have none he directed me to the Trollebotten Path."

Castillo didn't pay our way? I assumed that was part of our deal.

Chawett ground his teeth and shook his head. "This time of year the Trollebotten Path is infested with trolls. We might as well still be stuck back in the Maze if we have to take that route back. It will be dark by the time we reach the halfway point, the amount of trolls triple on that path at night."

"Castillo!" I yelled out. "We need to talk!"

Castillo and Gnarly came over to the arch where they stopped just before going under it. "My time is short," Castillo said. "What is it now Orcslaughter?"

"We need some of that perdants gold we acquired together to pay this toll."

Castillo looked at the elf leader and smirked. He pushed his finger into my chest. "Our deal was to bring your so-called questing team to the mouth of the entry cave. Nothing was said about the toll road, but I do have a proposition for you. Gnarly here needs a sniffer, I will pay your team's toll in trade for yours."

Gnarly reached her hands toward Mustela, who hissed and ducked behind Tigress' neck and hair.

Tigress stepped back with hands over her daggers. "Keep your filthy hands away from her you ratchet little freak."

Chawett plucked the cockatrice feathers from his hat. "I have something worth more than the sniffer to trade you Castillo. These feathers are from a Rex Goliath, they're worth a treasure trove of gold to the right wizard."

Castillo laughed. "Nice try, but you can keep your buzzard feathers Chawett. You all have got a whole lot to learn about the questing game." He turned and strutted back to join his team. "Have fun on the Trollebotten path. I'll be at Lais Dijon Tavern placing a heavy sum on a total slaughter bet for you fools!"

"And there it is," Chawett said. "Let's pick up the pace team, with a little hustle we just might make it more then half way to Trosworth before it gets too dark."

Chawett led the way speed-walking back to the entry cave. A right turn took us down the Trollbotton path. The trees took on a menacing look, despite the remaining sunshine.

"Once we get near the river crossing this road turns all bad," Chawett said. "I took this route with a twenty-five man questing team when it was snowing once. We lost three men to the six trolls we had to deal with on that run. In this weather we are sure to see quadruple the trolls I ran into that day. Our strategy is to be quick and unseen."

"Do you really think those feathers are worth something Chawett?" Tigress pulled her long hair over one shoulder to keep it from getting tangled in wandering tree branches.

"I do," he said. "If they are what I think they are. Some of the most wicked scrolls have been written with true Rex Goliath's."

Maybe it was a good thing we didn't trade them to Castillo.

"What do you mean by wicked?" Tigress asked wild-eyed.

"I once knew a wizard that needed a Rex feather to—"

Tigress held her arm out to block us. "What is that down the path?"

I skid to a halt and peered through the trees. Something tall, grey, and unmoving blocked the path far ahead. "It looks like a statue." Dread said.

"I don't recall any statues on the Trollbotten Path," Chawett said. "That's new."

"Let's investigate," I said.

Dread was the first to the stone figure. He looked it over then turned around with a smile. "That selfish serpent pulled the cockatrice head out the bag and looked at it. Chaz turned himself into stone!"

Chazekiel Manor had the heavylessness bag in one hand, and the cock head held up looking at it in the other. Chawett stood next to Dread admiring the sight. "I knew that severed cock's head would come in useful."

"Damn," I said. "If only the heavynessless bag, and everything in it hadn't turned to stone along with him."

Chawett walked right up on the statue. "I see one thing that *didn't* turn to stone." He pulled out his shillelagh, twirled and punched it down on Chaz's stone finger. The digit broke off the statue and fell to the ground. "Talhoffer's Ring of Enhanced Wizardry is still glistening gold baby!"

He strapped the shillelagh, picked up the finger by the ring and shook off the stone digit. Dread picked it up, and drop-kicked the finger deep into the forest.

"And the run once again bears fruit." I said. "We can trade the ring for passage down the toll road, and I hope a little gold on top."

Chawett held the prized Talhoffer item up. He then twisted it viewing all angles. "It would be a shame to do that. The elves don't value this stuff the way we do. This ring is worth over a hundred passes down the elf's road. I can put it on and use its power to fight off the trolls down our current path."

Tigress slid in front of Chawett and pushed down his hand. "Put that thing away for now, here comes the elf leader from the toll road."

"I see him," Chawett says. "Who's that other elf with him?"

The other elf was young-a boy. "That looks a lot like the little elf we rescued on the Carling Trail." I said.

"That is him!" Tigress said. "It's Tomte."

Tomte broke away from the leader, ran to Tigress, and wrapped around her waist with a hug. The elf leader joined them in conversation. I couldn't help but admire Tigress's smooth elfin speech-even though I understood none of it.

All three exchanged brief bows, then the leader and Tomte waved to us and went back toward the toll road.

"What was that about?" I asked.

Tigress' eyes smiled. "Tomte apologized for what happened to Chaz here."

"Well that was unnecessary," Dread said. "A stone Chaz is no loss off us."

"I know, right?" Tigress said. "When Chaz went to purchase passage down the toll road he ran into a problem. Tomte recognized him from the Carling trail and told his father how he wanted to leave him there for dead. Unfortunately for Chaz, Tomte's father is the elf leader, he wouldn't listen to a word Chaz had to say. After being denied passage down the toll road the traitor had no choice but to brave the Trollbotton path."

"Chaz did himself a favor by looking into that cock's eyes," Chawett said. "Dying at the hands of the trolls would have been a whole lot more painful."

Tigress grabbed my hand and pulled me back toward the toll road. "Come on team, the elf leader would like to reward us for saving his son. He will be providing a meal, and transportation on the owls to wherever we want to go. He also gave *me* an open invitation to come back and train with his band. I will have the opportunity to learn all the elfin fighting techniques. And guess what Dread? That includes extensive archery lessons."

"Well you definitely need that," Dread said. "No need to stand around here any longer, I'm hungry as a hostage, let's go get that meal."

The elves treated us to an enormous thank you lunch spread featuring the best greens the Light Woods had ever produced. Afterward Tomte pulled Tigress around the camp showing her off to all the members of his band. Mustela was a big hit with his younger friends. They stroked her fur as Tigress told the courageous story of the cockatrice fight.

Dread, Chawett, and I were made to feel right at home too. We got the pick of several choice wines the elf leader received in lieu of toll payments.

I broke away from the drinking to sit against a lonely oak tree and gather my thoughts. I rested my eyes for a brief moment when something gently pressed on my leg.

CHAPTER 25

I opened my eyes to see Porridge and her heart-warming smile. "Hey baby. I was worried about you in that Maze. I couldn't wait for you to come out." She laid across my lap and held me tight.

After dealing with all the death and hustle in the Maze this was just what I needed. I wrapped my arms around her frame. Holding Porridge made me feel it was all worth it. Even if I didn't find endless piles of gold on this run, I did find this fine thing I had in my arms right now.

"I was just daydreaming about you, pretty girl. It feels real good to be out of that Maze, especially with you in my arms. How did you find me? The last time I was blessed with your presence we were clear across these hills."

"The trees told me where you were."

"That's right, it's the dryad in you. I love that skill." I smoothed her hair away from her face to catch another glimpse of her eyes.

"The pixies gave me your message, thank you for freeing them."

"There was some dangerous stuff going on in that room they were locked up in. Rats, and fleas, and..." I trailed off. No need to think of the horrors now. We were out. Free. Poor, but free. "I hate to think what was going to happen to your friends. We found a whole lot of huo-yao in there too, just like Annabella said. Unfortunately it was turned to stone on our way out. I guess the Evons, and

Broxtonian's are safe from that whole pestilence thing you were worried about."

Porridge held my hand tight. "You are a hero Raff. The people on this island may never know, but the inhabitances of the Light Woods do, especially the pixies. It was an amazing sight to see them reunite with their families. Did you know two of those pixies were pregnant? You can look forward to receiving a hero's welcome from them."

She reached into her pocket. "I got a present for you." She pinned a small diamond shaped piece of bark under my collar. "This will gain you entrance to the Vic as an esteemed member of the alliance."

"The Vic, yes. Exotic accommodations are what you said they have there. When this run is over I would sure like to take you there for some get-to-know-each-other time. Do you think that'll be all right with your parents? They ran you out of that room at Tigress' house like a leprechaun to a pot of gold."

Porridge stood up with hands on hips. "You should know my father and step-mother like you. Remember, they cleaned your boots. If you take me out, I'll make you some more honey mint crisples for breakfast."

"So it was *you* who made those for me at the Questers Inn? You are sexy and can bake too. It's a date. But you have got to stop disappearing on me. I really hope one of those bottles on your belt has a sip of something that can take you to a tree in Beeston."

Porridge fidgeted with a small triangular bottle. "I don't have a connection with a Beeston tree yet. The bees there don't give them up easily."

Three giant owls swooped down into the elves camp. "Looks like my ride is here, have you ever ridden on an owl Porridge?"

"Oh no," she chuckled. "I've seen an elf or two fall off of those things, it's not a safe mode of travel."

"Raaaff!" Dread called me from a distance. "Raff come on, we getting ready to fly out."

Porridge stepped behind the oak tree. I looked for her but she was gone. *Blending into the trees with those brownie-dryad skills.*

Dread ran up to me. "Were you just fraternizing with an elf? I know they grateful for us saving little man, but damn. Where did she go?"

"You scared her off cousin," I said. "We were just starting to get cozy too."

"Tigress told me to come get you, the owls are ready to take us into Trosworth." He put one boot up on a bolder. "But first peep these."

Dreads old boots are gone. He now wore fine leather drawstring boots with 'D.J.' eloquently branded into them. "Little man's father made 'em for me." He stepped down and waltzed in a circle. "They're elfin thieves boots. Not only can I move silently in them, but it feels like I'm walking on featherbeds. My feet are happier than they have ever been, and my thief game is about to be a *problem!* Their doctor fixed my leg up too, using some concoction of juices and berries."

He raised both hands in the air and stretched out his fingers. "I feel like a new man all the way around. These wood elves are all right with me."

I packed my belongings extra tight and approached my owl. An elf helped me mount behind the pilot, and pulled a strap from the plumage. I tightened both hands around it with a death grip. The owls launched into the air flying low above the Light Woods. Looking down only the treetops were visible. At one point we flew through puffs of campfire smoke that rose from below. *Probably a group of questers on their way to the Maze.*

It was only a short while before we landed in a secluded area outside of Trosworth.

Tigress stroked her owls' head. "They will wait here for us to handle things in town."

Dread opened the door to Lais Dijon Tavern and led us to the gambling area. "I can't wait to see the look on William's face when he realizes we made it back alive."

A large crowd hovered at the moneychanger area. We walked up behind Castillo. He pushed a stack of gold coins to the clerk. "Max bet!"

He received a betting slip, and held it up high. "That's a bet! Five hundred gold coins says team Beeston gets totally slaughtered."

William walked up behind the clerk. Looked at me, then at Castillo. "You most definitely have a bet there Castillo."

"And I don't want no problems with the payout!" Castillo hollered. "Nine to one! There's *no* way them fools from Beeston are ever going to make it down the Trollebotten path alive."

I approached the scene with two fists in the air. "What it do William! Team Beeston checking in to collect in-and-outs."

Castillo turned around with his mouth gaping wide open. He ripped up the betting slip, threw the pieces in the air, and walked away through the falling confetti.

William laughed out laud. "You made it back! Looks like you're returning five of six too, not bad for your maiden run. Let me buy you all a round of drinks, I want to hear all about it."

"Were going to let Chawett tell our story," I said. "We got time-sensitive business back in Beeston."

William nodded his head. "Well I am going to have your names added to the board of accredited questers immediately. Remember, three successful in-and-outs can lead to big gold for a young quester around here."

A runner dropped a small sack in Williams hand. "And here you go Raff, your bet of five gold on the team Beeston under pays ten. Very swauve wagering my friend."

I looked at the team and winked. "I know a good bet when I see it."

We crossed the road to Moe's store. When we entered he was busy with two female customers.

"Let's look around until Moe concludes that business," Dread said. "I don't want to show off our goods."

Tigress grabbed Chawett's good hand. "Look over here, these are perfect for you." She pulled him toward some merchandise racks across from the counter.

Dread and I looked out the front window and watched the sun dip into the trees.

I saw the hag man working his hustle. "I will be right back cousin, I need to speak with somebody."

The man backed up when I approached. "I will *not* conduct business with you. It took me all night to get the hag back in her cage."

I'd tried to forget about what the hag did to me-an easy thing to do whilst in the Maze. But now that I had returned to a calmer reality, I needed to ask some questions. "Let me see her one more time, here's four gold coins for your trouble. I only need a few moments."

The man took the coins and draped an adder stone necklace over my head. "You're lucky it's been slow today."

Down in the dungeon I wrapped my fist around the adder stone. "Hag! Are you in there? What did you mean by I have to kill someone once a year? I need to know more about the magic."

The hag rose up on the bars with a twisted half-smile. "You smell of pixie and Cave Maze stench lover boy." She gargled up phlegm and chewed on it. "The catches involved with using your newly acquired magic is the least of your problems. I'm pregnant."

I squeezed the adder stone so hard it nearly cracked. "And what does that got to do with me?" A nasty twist took hold of my stomach.

The hag jammed her face between the bars. "Get me out of here, or your child will be born in this cage. That man up there will have her on display as an oddity for all to ridicule."

I ran my hand through my hair. This hag has got to be a lie. There is no way that incident could have led to a pregnancy. She was trying to throw me off when I needed answers about this magic. "How do I use the slip skin spell?"

"Fall asleep with your fingers intertwined above your chest. That's when you will be able to evoke the magic. You will have to kill somebody while you slip every once and a while or a sickness will envelop you. The amount of times you can slip, and must kill, depends on the strength of your lineage. I have answered your question. Now address your unborn child. Set me free and I will give birth to her in the comfort of my lair. If she is born hag you will never see me again. If it favors human you can have her."

"I don't believe any of this. I'm gone." I ran up the steps taking two at a time. This hag thought she could fool me?

"Dark magic is at work here!" The hag screeched. "Do me dirty and you-will-suffer!"

Outside of the door the man stood in front of me shaking his head. "You should see the look on your face."

I took off the stone, handed it to him, and started back across the street. Now that was one rotten lying hag. I might've had hag blood in me, but I had no magic. I would know if I had magic, it would feel good, enlightening. Not like this.

"Hey kid!" the man called. "That hag is full of half-truths, riddles, and calculated lies. She's quite a storyteller. But that's all they are... stories."

I hurried even faster across the street and opened Moe's door. The two ladies walked out.

Dread pulled my shirt. "Lets go handle this business so we can get back home. Time *is* of the essence." He semi-skipped over to Moe's counter. "My main man Moe. We're back."

"I knew you would be." Moe held up one finger and counted heads out loud. "One, two, three, four, five. You're returning five of six from the Maze. That means I was correct to bet the under. Thank you team Beeston. I knew you all would make it back with at least four. Hey, it's a good thing you gave me that deposit on the huo-yao sack. I just got those undercover hags to pay five hundred gold for theirs."

Dread looked back at me, straightened his collar, and then looked back at Moe. "My man! We'll definitely be concluding that deal for the huo-yao sack today. But first you got to see this." He looked back and stomped his foot. "Chawett, bring the goods. It's time."

Tigress chose a single leather glove from Moe's selection. She fitted it on Chawett's crinkled finger hand.

Chawett held out the freshly gloved hand and wiggled his nubs. "It's a snug fit. With this glove on, my hand almost looks like it could be normal."

Dread drummed his fingers on the counter. "Moe, you *are* truly my main man. I am going to give you first opportunity to purchase a few treasures we acquired on our run." He was laying it on a bit thick.

Moe raised an eyebrow and scanned the four of us. He slapped his hands down flat on the counter. "Well let's do business then. Let me see what you got."

Chawett laid the feathers on the counter, followed by the ring, which he concealed a bit with his good hand. I could understand his hesitance to give it up. Better focus on the small game first. "I believe these are authentic Rex Goliaths."

Moe skimmed his fingers over the feathers. It took him a moment to catch a breath. "And what of the ring?"

Chawett nodded his head slowly. "That would be Talhoffer's gold Ring of Enhanced Wizardry."

Moe leaned back and squinted. "Usually maze fresh Talhoffer items are contained in a nice oak box. Where is it?"

I stepped up to the counter. "It was damaged in transit. Look Moe, these are authentic as could be."

He looked closely at both items. "The feathers are consistent with Goliaths I've seen before, but this ring doesn't look like one of Talhoffer's personal magic items to me." Moe pinched the ring, lifted it up, and looked through the middle. "What you got here is a nice piece of Cave Maze treasure, but it's a ring that has no magic power."

So why didn't it turn to stone when Chaz got petrified? Was Moe trying to cheat us or did he really believe it was worthless? Chawett pressed his lips together. "Lets just go through the authentication process before we rush to judgment Moe."

"Okay." Moe reached under the counter and brought up a porcelain inkwell. It was the figure of a mange dog urinating into a bucket. "Dipping your feathers into albino bat's blood will tell us the true story here." He dipped the tip of a feather into the black liquid contained in the bucket, lifted it, and let a drop fall off onto the ring.

Moe held the feather up high with the tip down and blew on it from top to bottom. He stared at it for a moment then shook his head. "Nothing's happening." He looked down at the ring. "Nothing's happening to either item."

Tigress pushed her way to the counter. "What are you looking for them to do Moe?"

His bottom lip protruded out. "If magic was present in these items something would happen. I can give you thirty gold coins for the ring. I don't want the feathers. There's just no magic here."

"Let me try a puff." Tigress licked her lips and gently blew on the feather's tip. It instantly shot upward out of Moe's hand. A faint trail of purple glitter smoke smoldered as it floated back to the table.

Moe wiped his hand across his face and smiled big. "You got some magical lips. It's authentic, and that purple smoke indicates it's of the highest quality. I can give you five hundred gold coins for each feather."

"Not enough," Chawett said. "I personally know magic users who will pay double that for purple Goliaths. Nine hundred per is what we need."

Moe pushed the feathers away. "Put want in one hand, gold in the other, then tell me which one weighs more. I've got gold coins right here and now. I'll go up to six hundred each, no more."

"Nobody's brought purple Goliaths to market for a long time Moe," Chawett said. "I know wizards tend to salivate over purples. Do eight hundred and they're yours. I really don't want to ask around the tavern for a buyer."

Moe's eyes darted between the feathers. Chawett was making him nervous. That boded well for us. "I'll pay seven hundred and fifty. I got real gold coins just a few seconds away from your hand."

"It's a deal," Chawett said. "Seven-fifty each."

Moe ducked under the counter and stacked up our gold payment.

"There you go, fifteen hundred gold."

Dread hovered over the coins. "Now that's what I'm talking about. Looks like my first purchase with this gold will have to be one of those heavynesless bags. My pockets are going to burst under all this booty."

Moe scooped up the feathers. "So why don't you blow on this ring for me young lady? Let's see if anything magical happens."

I snatched the ring off the counter. "You're probably correct about the ring Moe. For thirty gold I'd just as soon keep it. We will need that huo-yao sack, four heavynessless bags, and the glove on Chawett's hand."

I led the team out of Moe's store to the street.

"What's on your mind Raff?" Dread asked. "I was ready to see what kind of gold we could get for that ring. You already know it's a real Talhoffer item."

"Before I get into that I have a question for our magic user. Chawett, how good are your magic powers going to be now that you only have five digits?"

Chawett struggled to make a fist with his newly gloved hand. "My Cave Maze useful magic was shaky with all ten of my fingers in tact. With only five, no accredited questing team will touch me."

"I'm thinking that total slaughter bet William posted would have paid out real big if it weren't for you on our team. You saved our lives several times on this run. Dread, Tigress, I say we split the gold from the feathers amongst the three of us, and pay Chawett off with the ring. Would that be all right with you Chawett?"

Chawett cracked a huge smile. "That would be more than all right! You would do that for me?"

"You know we wouldn't have it any other way," Dread said. "Chawett you are truly my main magic man."

Tigress put her hand on my shoulder. "I love that idea Raff. Chawett, thank you for everything you did down there."

Chawett looked down at his gloved hand. "The ring will change everything for me. Wearing it will not only cancel out the negative effect of having burnt fingers, but it will increase my magic to the wizard level immediately. I will be a top ranked magic user in no time with the ring on any one of my five remaining fingers."

I dug the ring out from my pocket and held it up between my finger and thumb. "This is yours then Chawett. But you have to promise to be team Beeston's magic user when we return to the Maze."

Chawett took off his hat and bowed our direction. "When Beeston's best return, I'm your magic user."

Tigress stood in front of me with her hand out. I laid the ring in her palm. "Bless him with it Tigress."

She slid the ring on Chawett's finger. His eyes jolted into the back of his head. He jerked five times then stood calmly.

"How do you feel?" Tigress asked.

Chawett removed the glove to reveal five regenerated fingers. He rubbed his hands together creating a cantaloupe-sized lava sphere. With a swipe of his hands he flicked the sphere straight up into the air. A thunderous crack echoed through the valley. "Oh yes! That's how a wizard does it!"

⚔ CHAPTER 26 ⚔

We waved good-bye to Chawett as the owls took flight. I'd miss that guy. Already, I itched for another Cave Maze run.

"I hope these owls get us home fast," Dread said. "We only have until sunrise for our meeting with Joe. If my dad isn't up for a late night session, we'll be in deep neck-slitting trouble."

"I know that's right." I hunkered down on the owl. "Tigress, can you let our pilots know that time is of the essence?"

"You just did," she said.

From below, Chawett thrust six spheres high into the air lighting up our way. The owls took a swift turn then dove downwind toward Beeston.

I could just make out dense puffs of smoke coming up from under Uncle Mack's porch. When the owls swooped down he stood up from his favorite chair.

Dread jumped off his ride first. "Dad, we got the huo-yao."

Mack stepped to the edge of the porch. He dropped his pipe and rubbed his eyes with both hands. "Are you riding an owl? With elves?"

Dread held up the sack of huo-yao and shook it. "Never mind that, did you hear me? We got the huo-yao."

"That's my boy." Mack said. "Bring that on in here son. I'll get the paraphernalia ready." He turned and made his way into the house.

"Remember Dread," I said. "We need those busters put together quick, there're only a few hours until our deadline with Joe." Despite the rush, our deadline seemed like a minor challenge compared to what we already overcame.

Dread picked up his father's fallen pipe, took a puff, and blew the smoke in a slow steady stream my direction. "I know." He then smiled and waved. "Bye Tigress, bye Mustela." He ducked into the house behind his dad.

Mustela jumped on my shoulder and licked my face. Tigress smiled. "Thank you for including me on this insane run Raff. I made more than enough gold to pay off all of our debt and purchase a new breeding sniffer. After I take care of things at home, I just might take the elves up on their offer to train me. Will you be available to escort Mustela and me back to the elves when I'm ready?"

"You two were great in the Maze, and I'll escort you to the edge of the earth if you want me to." Should I tell her about our connection?

"One good thing about you escorting me back there is that you would be able to see that elf girl I saw you hugged up on again."

The very mention of Porridge-despite Tigress thinking she was an elf-made me want to jump on an owl again and speed back to her. "Oh, about that—"

"No need for explanations Raff. You're a player just like your father, and I know it. Besides, dating you would be like dating my brother."

Imagine that. "We got a lot to talk about on that trip back to the elves Tigress. How do you feel about hooking me up with that brownie girl from your house?"

"There you go again Raff. I guess your father would be proud. I don't play matchmaker."

Tigress kissed me on the cheek then jumped on her owl. I missed her as soon as she was in the air.

"Nephew!" Uncle Mack called out. "Stop playing the kissing game out there and come on in. We need some help to make these busters."

I took a seat at the table. There was a scattered mess of various papers, tools, and strings used in the making of our explosives.

"The master is at work." I said.

"So did you get a kiss from that pretty little Tigress before she flew away?" Mack asked.

"Yah Raff," Dread added. "Did you get a little somethin' somethin' or not?"

I sifted through the sack of huo-yao. "It isn't like that between us. She's like my sister."

Mack coughed and patted his chest. "I'll let you tell it, nephew." He scooped up some huo-yao and spread it across custom paper.

Several hours later Uncle Mack rolled up the ninth buster. "Voila! Your neck-saving order is ready. Get up and go on you two."

Dread swung by the table and scooped up the package. "No time to waste, let's get it."

⸸ ⸸ ⸸

As Dread unlocked our shop door, I looked over Village Square. With the sun coming up a bee flew by me on its way up into the trees. The buzzing seamed to vibrate through me. I really missed hearing the bees morning buzz. *It's good to be home.*

As I hoisted the window several horses arrived. Joseph stormed in the door. "Well, well, well. I did *not* expect to see you boys here this morning. Do you have my product?"

Dread handed Joseph the bundle. "Here you go my man. Nine explosives, as promised."

Joseph slammed the package on a table and snatched out a buster. He pinched it in the middle and sniffed it from end-to-end. "These are fluffy, just the way I like them. Some rumors out of Chilwell said that you two headed up a questing team. I was worried you might not make it out of there alive to provide me with my order."

He wrapped up the package. "I apologize for the whole dagger to the throat thing Dread, but as we all know, you can never trust a

Jenkins."

I shook Joseph's hand and smiled. "Well, being a Jenkins is exactly what kept us alive on our run. The family name has some unpredicted pull in the field."

Dread took a seat on our bench, nodded his head and smiled. "Well-said cousin."

"I need to place another order," Joseph said.

Dread perked up. "I will have ten more fluffy busters just like those available in three days."

"Good," Joseph said. "I'll be needing more."

Another rider slid to a noisy stop in front of the shop. Jeevesekial Manor busted in and unsheathed his sword. "So its true. Team Beeston is back, but my brother is not! If anything bad happened to Chazsekial there will be a price to pay, and it won't be payable in gold coins."

"Damn your cowardice brother," Dread said.

Jeeves scowled, raised his sword, and started toward Dread. Joseph pushed Jeeves back. "You know the rules of the Cave Maze game. If your brother didn't make it out, then he didn't make it out. We all know how death stacks up in there."

Dread stood with a throwing spike in each hand. He cocked one arm back in position. "Let him go Joe. We can settle this like cavaliers, or get into some dirty thief tactics. The choice is yours Jeeves, I'm right here."

Joseph stared at Chaz's disgruntled brother and pointed outside. "Get on the road Jeeves. This is not how Questing University team members deal with Cave Maze death."

Jeevesekial stormed out but turned around at the door. "I'm on my way into Trosworth where I will get to the bottom of this. If I get word there was any foul play you two jesters are dead." He pulled a scroll from his pocket. "That is if I can get to you first."

I was fresh out the Cave Maze. This blowhard didn't scare me.

He unrolled the scroll. "An ass-centaur has been posting these all over Broxington. According to this, Talhoffer is offering a reward for the head of one Raff Orcslaughter. Apparently Orcslaughter has stolen Talhoffer's complete stash of huo-yao, and sabotaged a weapon that the good wizard says was sure to wipe out the Evons, and their threat of invasion. Anyone aiding the Evons is an enemy of us all. I wonder if *you* have any relation to this other Raff?"

"Never heard of him," I said.

Jeeves' eyes incinerated with disgust. "We will see. Talhoffer is missing huo-yao, and you just delivered huo-yao explosives. I don't think that's a coincidence." He rode away laughing.

Just as Dread and I walked Joseph out of the shop door Chancellor Liberi trotted up. "Joseph, what's the matter here? We need to be on our way."

Joseph patted me on the back and mounted his horse. "I was just congratulating these young questers on there first in-and-out of the Maze."

"I got a question for you Mr. Liberi," I said. "Are you still accepting new students?"

The Chancellor looked at me with a furrowed brow. "I am."

"Well then I would like to enroll. I can pay my entire first year's tuition up front." I held a sack of gold up to the Chancellor. "The Cave Maze was *very* good to me, sir."

"I am well aware of your fighting skills Raff," Liberi said. "A freshman student with an official in-and-out will be a first at my institution." He accepted the sack then tossed it to a rider behind him. "Consider yourself enrolled at Questing University, Raff Jenkins. I will see you on campus in twelve days."

Joseph, Chancellor Liberi, and their entourage trotted off toward Trosworth.

Dread put his hand on my shoulder. "I'm thinking the story of Chaz's petrification will not sit well with Jeeves. You're sure to have some problems with that bully at the university."

"Damn him," I said. "Chaz got what he deserved. Now let's go get what we deserve, some of that good honey mead."

As I helped Dread lock the shop door a familiar female voice came from behind us. "Don't you think it's too early in the morning for a drink?"

I turned around, picked Porridge up, and gave her a long kiss while I spun her in a circle. "I am crazy in love with you right now girl. And that's just how we celebrate here in Beeston, drinks all day."

I didn't ask how she got here. I didn't ask where she'd been. Frankly…I didn't care. She was here and she was mine.

"Well show me the way boo." she said.

"Who is this girl Raff?" Dread asked in his high voice. "And does she have any friends that look just like her?"

I put my arm around Porridge and started towards the Skeppers Pub. "I'll tell you all about this pretty young thing over that well-deserved victory drink cousin."

"Victory *drink* Raff?" Dread asked. "You mean two, three, four, or more victory *drinks* my man. The questers of team Beeston are coming to celebrate!"

THE END

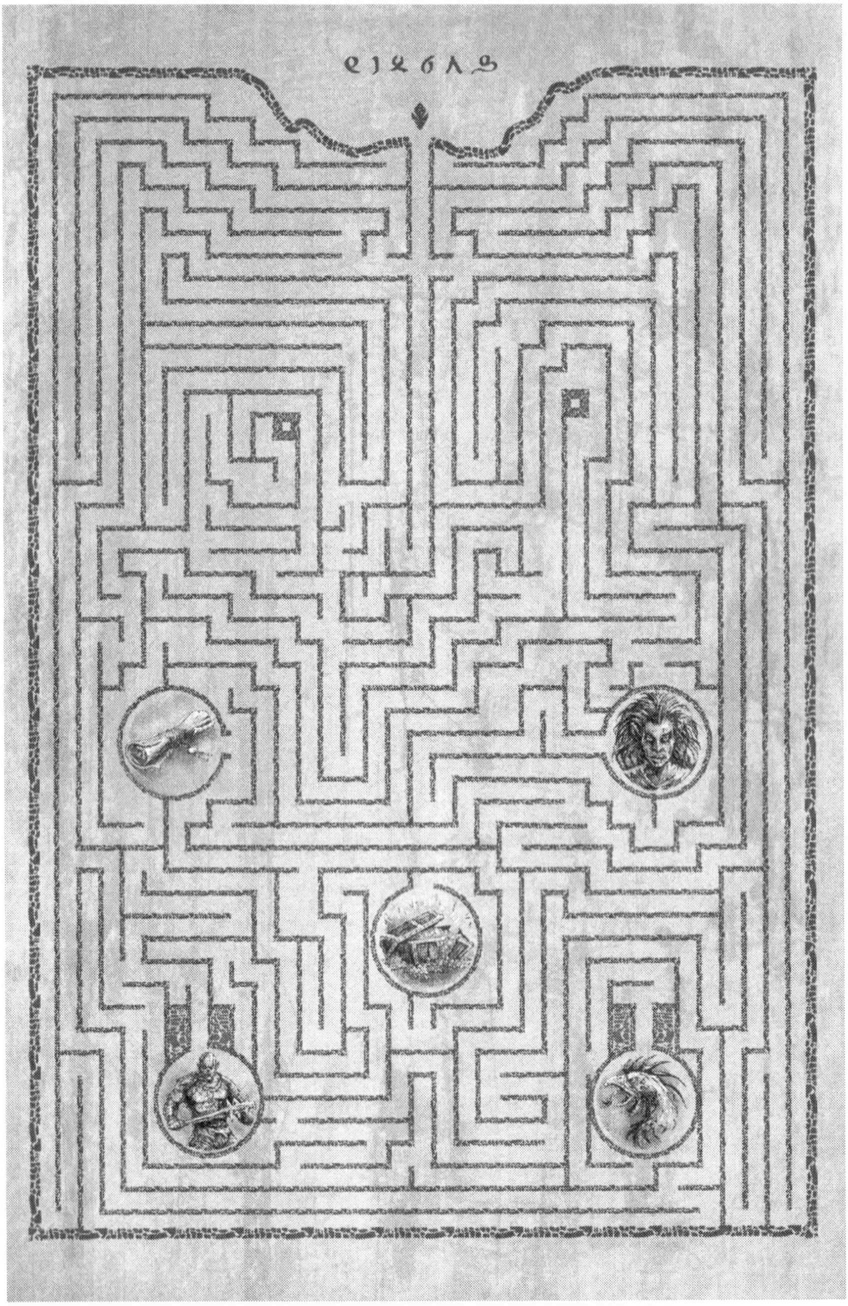

ABOUT THE AUTHOR

C. A. A. Allen lives in San Diego with his wife and six children. He is a freelance writer, local hip-hop mogul, and fantasy e-book author. He writes for many online entities, and has been published in the San Diego Reader, and CityBeat magazines. He has provided back up vocals, and performed as a "Humpty Dancer" for the multi-platinum hip-hop group Digital Underground. When he isn't writing or spending time with his children, Mr. Allen enjoys horse racing, fine cognac, funk music, and southern cooking. *The Cave Maze*, is his debut novel.

Visit him online: www.facebook.com/CaveMaze

Facebook: TheCaveMaze

Twitter: @TheCaveMaze

THE CAVE MAZE
WIZARD WARRIOR QUEST
C.A.A. ALLEN

COLLECT THE MAP AND TAKE THE TREASURE

FANTASTIC SCIENCE
FANTASY ADVENTURES
PRESS

Made in the USA
Charleston, SC
14 October 2015